THE
MIRRABROOK
MARRIAGE

THE
MIRRABROOK
MARRIAGE

BY

BARBARA HANNAY

MILLS & BOON®

First published in Great Britain 2005
Large Print edition 2005
Harlequin Mills & Boon Limited,
Eton House, 18-24 Paradise Road,
Richmond, Surrey TW9 1SR

© Barbara Hannay 2005

ISBN 0 263 18594 X

Set in Times Roman 17½ on 19½ pt.
16-1005-42089

Printed and bound in Great Britain
by Antony Rowe Ltd, Chippenham, Wiltshire

CHAPTER ONE

SARAH ROSSITER loved Southern Cross.

She was never happier than when she was riding over rust-red plains on a strong and beautiful horse. She loved to look up to a cobalt-blue sky billowing above her like an enormous mainsail and to hear the thud of thousands of hooves pounding through thick creamy-gold kangaroo grass.

Most of all she loved to be on a cattle muster with Reid McKinnon, working the mob with him, steering the cattle out of the stands of black-trunked ironbarks and pushing them across the Star Valley towards the holding yards.

And yet, working with Reid was exactly what she shouldn't be doing.

This year she'd actually made a solemn pledge to decline politely if he invited her to join in another muster. Heaven knew she had plenty of good excuses. As the sole teacher in charge of all seven year levels at Mirrabrook's tiny primary school, she had enough on her plate without giving up precious weekends to help out with cattle.

But Reid had driven into town late one afternoon, just as she was closing up the classroom. With his thumbs hooked through the loops of his jeans, he'd hitched a lean hip against the railing of the little school's wooden veranda and he'd flashed that shiver-gorgeous smile of his and had asked ever so casually if she would be free for a muster the following weekend. And she'd said yes.

Just like that. No hesitation. She'd looked into his silver-grey eyes and her brain had gone straight into meltdown. *Again.*

'Yes, Reid, sure I can help. I'd love to.'
Fool.

Later, she'd tried to justify her weakness. She told herself that she'd only agreed to help Reid because his sister Annie was still away in Italy and his brother Kane had moved over to Lacey Downs with his new English bride, which left Southern Cross short-handed. But she knew jolly well that Reid could manage without her. He would almost certainly be hiring contract musterers to make up the numbers.

Reid had suggested that Sarah was invaluable because she knew the country so well; she could comb the bush for stray cattle without getting lost. But that wasn't why she'd come. Truth was, it didn't really matter what reasons he offered, she would have agreed to help out under any circumstances. Sarah was weak as water where Reid was concerned. She had been that way for the past ten years.

Ten years. *Ouch!* It was so scary to think that she'd wasted a decade of her life, from the age of seventeen to twenty-seven—the years when a young woman was supposed to be at her most beautiful and alluring—

waiting for Reid McKinnon to come to his senses and acknowledge that he loved her.

Although...if she was fair and completely honest, she would admit that those ten years hadn't been a total waste of time...more like a very long, progressively steep learning curve.

But the end result was her painful realisation that what had begun as a wonderful friendship and had blossomed into a beautiful romance between herself and Reid hadn't stood the test of time.

Something had gone wrong. Something irrevocable. Something that seemed to have hurt Reid terribly.

Whatever had happened, it was so deeply painful that he'd never been able to explain it to her, even though there had been times when she'd been certain he wanted to tell her. She hadn't pushed him for answers because she'd sensed that challenging him would have made things worse and be distressing for them both. Her strategy had been to accept second best—Reid's friendship instead of his love—in the hope that he just needed time.

And here she was, taking part in yet another cattle muster on Southern Cross, simply because Reid had invited her.

A sudden shout ahead caught her attention. Reid was signalling with a wave of his Akubra hat that it was time to close in on the herd and to keep them compact. This meant that the leading cattle must be within sight of the yards now.

Panicking cattle often tried to break away as they neared the gate, so it was time to forget her foolish heartache and to concentrate on the job at hand. Time for the cattle dogs to show their mettle, working extra hard as they edged the mob forward.

Reid would man the gate, while the two ringers positioned themselves on either side. Sarah's role was to stay at the rear of the herd, ready to round up any breakaways.

Over the backs of the sea of cattle, she watched the effortless grace with which Reid dismounted, an action as natural as breathing for a man of the outback. Once he was on the ground she could only see a shoulder-high view of him—of his battered Akubra and his blue shirt straining over hard-packed muscles as he tethered his horse. Then she heard the rattle of the gate being opened.

Keeping her horse on the move, she weaved back and forth, nudging the stragglers to stay with the mob. Only when everything seemed to be proceeding smoothly did she let her thoughts roll forward to what would happen next, after this muster.

Reid would invite her up to the homestead to join him and the ringers for an evening meal. But should she accept this time as she had every other time?

It was always pleasant to stop off at the homestead to take a shower and rid herself of layers of dust before heading back into town to her own little house. And it was more than pleasant to spend a couple of hours in Reid's company, sharing a meal and conversation, a drink or two and a laugh or three. But these days it was bittersweet torment too.

Surely she'd put herself through that kind of misery one time too many. At some point very soon she would have to—

A flash of tan to her right cut through her thoughts. A beast had turned and bolted and now others were following. And she'd been caught napping.

To Sarah's shame her mount, Jenny, a well-trained stock horse, reacted before she did. *Darn.* Once again she'd let Reid McKinnon mess with her head and now her pride was at stake. No jillaroo worth her salt let cattle escape at this final stage of a muster.

Precious seconds late, she pressed her knees into Jenny's flanks and crouched low in the saddle as the horse took off after the escapees.

More by good luck than good management she caught up with the leader before the breakaways reached the heavy timbers. Then it was a matter of thinking and acting quickly. Turning her horse in an instant, she drew on all her riding skills to change direction often and fast until at last she'd rounded them up.

To her relief the cattle gave in and trotted obediently back towards the main mob. And Sarah refused to give Reid McKinnon another moment's thought until the last beast was fenced in.

The sun was slipping westward by the time the job was done. The ringers stayed down at the yards, making sure the cattle were calm and, as the last of the coppery light lingered, Sarah and Reid walked the four horses up to the saddling enclosure.

There they removed the saddles and washed the horses' backs and gave them a small feed of grain. Sarah concentrated on giving the animals the very best attention and she tried hard not to take any special notice of Reid working nearby.

Tried not to watch the neat way his well-worn faded jeans hugged his behind as he bent down to examine one of the horses' shoes. Tried not to steal glimpses of his muscular forearms or his strong tanned hands as they stroked a horse's neck. Especially, she tried not to remember how those hands had once caressed her intimately, bringing her the piercing sweet pleasure of a lover's touch.

No! she chastised herself. She had to get over it and get over him!

Shaking her head at her own hopelessness, she hurried to stow the saddles in the tack room. Why couldn't she just accept that Reid wasn't interested in her?

For him, their past had never happened; they had never been uninhibited, ecstatic, totally smitten lovers.

Under the guise of friendship, he'd continued to partner her to local balls and charity dos that raised money for the Flying Doctors, or the School of the Air. Every so often he would amble in to town to buy her a coffee at Beryl's café, or a drink at the pub. And on odd occasions he called in at her place on the way home from a day's fishing on the river and delivered a fish or two. He'd even filleted them and cooked them for her.

And she had been pathetically grateful for whatever crumbs of friendship he threw her way.

Problem was—and for Sarah it was a *huge* problem—her major stumbling block—there were other times when she was just as certain that Reid was still attracted to her—deeply.

There were times when he'd taken her home from a ball or a party and they'd said goodnight and she'd sensed a terrible tension between them. Times when Reid had looked at her—*looked* at her—with a breath-robbing mixture of despair and longing that was impossible to misinterpret.

But he hadn't kissed her. He'd always covered the awkward moment with a joke and then turned quickly and hurried back to his vehicle.

Those moments had caused her too many sleepless nights.

Now, as she stepped back through the tack room doorway, Reid turned and he looked straight towards her and he seemed to freeze. He stood rock still in the middle of the yard, staring at her.

It was happening again.

That hunger in his eyes wasn't a fantasy conjured by her overwrought imagination. The feverish heat and dark longing were real. And her poor heart felt as if it had taken off for the moon.

Deep colour stained Reid's cheekbones. His chest rose and fell as if he'd suddenly run out of breath and his face was a mirror of the same deep yearning she felt for him.

The sight of it unleashed a terrible tumult inside her. The usual tumult. Each time this happened it trapped her afresh. Each time she hoped that *this* time Reid would haul her into his arms and show her with his body what he couldn't tell her. Show her the truth…that he loved her still.

This time…

It had to happen. Had to be this time.

They couldn't go on like this. It was hopeless.

Hopeless…

Hopeless. The hollow, desolate word echoed and clanged in her head.

Perhaps it was that empty echo or perhaps it was the effect of the afternoon sunlight, gilding Reid with a bronzed glow that made him more unbearably handsome than ever. Whatever the reason, Sarah suddenly knew that this had to be a turning point.

A man who looked at a woman with that kind of hunger should push her against a wall and kiss her for a week. He should grab her and haul her down into the hay bales in the corner of the yard. She wouldn't allow Reid to look at her as if he wanted to make love to her and dismiss the moment with another grin, another joke.

If he did…she had no choice; she would walk away from him today and not come back. She would leave the district—apply for a transfer and take a teaching post in another part of the state. Reclaim her life.

Her heart thumped painfully as she watched him stoop to pick up his saddle. She didn't move as he began to stride across the yard towards her and she couldn't help running her tongue over her lips to rid them of dust.

His eyes followed the movement and hungry shadows darkened his silver irises. He drew close and she held her breath.

Just toss that saddle aside and kiss me, Reid. I'm yours. You know I've always been yours.

A breathless hush seemed to fall over the bush as he stopped in front of her. It was so quiet she could hear the pounding rhythm of her blood drumming in her veins.

He stopped so close in front of her that she could see the individual grains of skin on his strong jaw and the tiny pinprick beginnings of his dark beard.

This is your last chance, Reid.

Behind him, one of the horses made a soft snuffling snort.

The sound seemed to break the spell. Reid's mouth tilted into a lopsided smile.

And Sarah's heart sank straight through the hard-packed dirt of the horse yard.

'You've got a leaf caught in your hair,' he said, reaching with his free hand to pluck something from a dark strand that hung over her shoulder.

She closed her eyes and her chest squeezed the breath from her lungs as his hand brushed close to her cheek without quite touching. She felt the flick of his fingers against her hair and the brush of his wrist on her shoulder, but when she dared to open her eyes again he was moving past her to set the saddle inside the tack room.

She knew that when he returned the dark emotion in his eyes would be replaced by a milder light and he would be smiling easily.

But no.

When he stepped outside he paused again, standing beside her, staring with an intensity that made her tremble. She felt ill. If it didn't happen now, it never would.

Muscles in his throat worked and he looked away. 'We'd better go up to the homestead.'

Beside him Sarah had to reach for the door frame to steady herself. She felt so drained she couldn't even cry.

Reid frowned. 'You're coming up to the house, aren't you, Sarah?'

She tried to swallow the clump of awful emotion in her throat. 'I don't think I will today, thanks.'

His eyes pierced her with a sharp, searching wariness. 'Don't you want to sample our new cook's fare? He's very good.'

She shrugged in an effort to hide the storm breaking inside her. 'I still have some marking to do and lessons to prepare for next week.' Before she could weaken, she set off across the yard. 'Catch you later, Reid.'

He didn't respond.

She told herself that it was a good sign; she'd shocked him. But when she reached the gate and turned to wave goodbye she caught a glimpse of his stricken face as he stared at the ground, and his clear disappointment gave her no sense of satisfaction. None at all.

*   *   *

'You're leaving town?' Ned Dyson, the editor of Mirrabrook's tiny newspaper, couldn't have looked more appalled if Sarah had announced she'd contracted smallpox.

'I'm afraid so, Ned. I've applied to the Education Department for a transfer to the coast. I'm well overdue for a change, so I'm pretty confident they'll let me go.'

Ned groaned and threw his arms into the air in a melodramatic gesture of despair. Next moment he launched himself out of his swivel chair, circuited his paper-strewn desk and came to a halt in front of Sarah. Pushing his glasses back up his ski slope nose, he stared at her as if he needed to look into her eyes before he'd believe her.

'Do you really want to go? After all this time?'

She nodded. She was determined to go through with this. She had to.

Ned let out a noisy sigh and propped his hands on his hips. 'The town's going to take this hard, Sarah.'

'I suppose they might, but that's only because I've been here for too long and everyone's so used to me.'

'It's more than that. We'll never get another teacher who loves the kids the way you do.'

'Of course you will.'

'And what about your agony aunt column?' Ned raked a pudgy hand over his bald patch and his eyes bulged with horror. 'Geez, Sarah, I've Buckley's chance of finding anyone who can hand out advice the way you do. You've got such a knack. The whole district hangs on to your every word.'

But now it's time for me to take my own advice.

'What I write is just common sense, Ned. You know that.'

'But you always manage to make people feel so good about themselves—even when they've made stupid mistakes.' Ned flung out his arms. 'You're a flaming genius. Most people around here think I hire someone from down south to answer their letters, some hotshot psychologist in the big smoke.'

'That's not because I'm any kind of genius; it's because they want to believe the advice is coming from an expert. We both know they'd be devastated if they discovered the woman who taught their kids was Ask Auntie.'

'Doesn't matter. You're damn good.'

Sarah dropped her gaze to avoid the pleading in Ned's eyes. Nothing about her move away was going to be easy. For starters, she didn't really want to go. It would be a wrench to turn her back on her little school; she would miss her seventeen pupils terribly. She loved every one of them—even the naughty ones—*especially* the naughty ones.

And she knew the Mirrabrook townsfolk would be sorry to lose her; she'd become so much a part of their lives, but if she was going to reclaim her life she had to make a clean break from Reid.

'It's time for me to go, Ned. It's been a hard decision, but in the end I—I don't have much choice.'

He frowned and looked as if he was waiting for an explanation. When she didn't offer any he asked, 'What about Reid? What's he had to say?'

It was weird the way people who knew her well still thought of Reid as her boyfriend. In this town they were still Sarah-and-Reid—a proper courting couple who were probably going to be married some day. How could anyone miss the glaringly obvious truth?

She managed a half-hearted smile and shrugged. 'Reid's cool.' Then, before Ned could comment, she rushed to ask, 'Did you get the Ask Auntie responses I emailed through to you for this week?'

'Yeah, thanks. I haven't had a chance to read them yet, but I'm sure they're okay.' He cast an eye over the mess of papers on his desk, then grimaced and patted his paunch as if he had indigestion. 'The paper's circulation is going to drop when you go.'

'Don't panic just yet, Ned. You've time to think about a replacement. I won't be going till the end of the school term.'

He brightened a little. 'That means you'll still be here for Annie McKinnon's wedding?'

'Yes.' Flinching inwardly, Sarah forced a smile as she remembered the excited phone call she'd received a couple of months earlier from Annie in Rome. She summoned a deep, calming breath to still the awful jealousy she felt every time she thought about Annie's wedding. Why had both Kane and Annie McKinnon taken to the idea of marriage like ducks to the Star River, while Reid…?

No, she wouldn't waste another thought in that direction. 'Annie's asked me to be a bridesmaid.'

Ned grinned. 'That's great. You'll be a ter-
rific bridesmaid.'

'I won't be the only bridesmaid, of
course. Annie has a couple of friends in
Brisbane she's asked to do the honours,
too.'

Ned beamed. 'Better and better. I'll bet
they're good sorts.' He rubbed his hands together as if he'd just been struck by a brilliant idea. 'I reckon a McKinnon wedding
is a big enough stir in this little valley to
make the front page of the *Mirrabrook Star*,
don't you?'

'I reckon it is, Ned.' Sarah tried for another smile but couldn't quite manage it.

Later that evening, Sarah took a pad and
pencil through to her study, a converted
back bedroom in her little house beside the
school in Mirrabrook's main street. It was a
little old Queenslander cottage, the standard
design built forty years ago by the
Education Department and she'd made it
her own little haven.

Over the years she'd collected a modest assortment of antiques, handicrafts and artwork, including a handmade quilt on a wall in her lounge room, North Queensland pottery vases filled with native flowers, a bed with antique brass ends covered by a white hand-crocheted bedspread, and a couple of original paintings.

Sarah loved to surround herself with beautiful things. They lifted her spirits. Most of the time.

She doubted anything would cheer her tonight. It was time to make a list of all the things she wanted to take with her when she moved.

But she'd barely started before she found herself surrounded by memories, and suddenly the task seemed much harder than it should have been. Just looking at the cork board above her desk brought painful waves of nostalgia.

Every photo, every memo or scrap of paper with lines from a song was a poignant link to a significant memory. Good grief, there was even the programme from the last Speech Night she'd attended at boarding school.

That was the night she'd met Reid. When she was just seventeen.

Reaching up now, she pulled out the drawing pin that secured the programme to the board. It had been there so long it left a rusty ring around the pinprick.

She should have taken it down ages ago of course. The fact that it was still there was a very obvious symptom of her pathetic reluctance to let go of hopeless dreams.

Bending down to toss it in the basket under her desk, she hesitated. Big mistake. In spite of her resolve to forget, memories rushed back.

And, heaven help her, she let them... Suddenly she wanted to remember it all... just one more time.

Sinking into her deep swivel chair, she let the memories come.

CHAPTER TWO

SARAH met Reid in the School Hall where everybody gathered for supper after the Speech Night presentations. Because she was School Captain and had delivered a farewell speech to her fellow students that evening, she was kept busy for ages while everyone from the local mayor to the school gardener congratulated her.

Which was all very nice, but by the time she escaped to the long trestle tables where tea and coffee and cakes were served there was nothing left. Boarding school girls were piranhas around food.

Draining a heavy teapot, she managed half a cup of cool, brewed tea and found a dubiously thin slice of very boring sponge cake, minus its icing.

'It's a grim turnout when the most important girl in the school can't even find a cup of tea,' a male voice said close behind her.

Even before she turned around she knew the speaker was smiling; she could hear it in the warmth in his voice. Just the same, when she turned to look over her shoulder she wasn't prepared for the full effect of that smile.

Oh, wow! Talk about gorgeous!

He had to be in his mid-twenties, which immediately set him apart from the schoolboys of her acquaintance. Tall, dark and, yes, yummy looking too—he had the bronzed, outdoorsy skin and athletic physique of a man of the land. And the most wonderful, iridescent, silver-grey eyes.

The moment she looked into them Sarah felt as if she'd zoomed straight into the stratosphere. *Far out!* If only she wasn't wearing her school uniform! What a bummer to meet such a scrumptious guy when she was stuck in a crummy blazer, shapeless white blouse and tie, teamed with a too-long ugly grey pleated skirt.

Not that the clothes seemed to put him off.

'We should be able to find someone to make you a fresh pot of tea,' he said.

She dragged her eyes from him to cast a quick glance around the supper tables. 'I can't see any of the kitchen staff here.'

Without hesitation he picked up one of the huge metal teapots. His eyes sparkled with merriment and she fancied she caught the ghost of a wink. 'Let's go and hunt them down then. Which way is the kitchen?'

She gasped—not because there was anything particularly shocking about the stranger's suggestion, but because she was so stunned that he was obviously using the lack of tea as an excuse to chat her up. But heavens, why not let him? Here she was, on the brink of leaving school, on the eve of womanhood, and she'd just looked into his eyes and seen a glimpse of a beckoning, enticing new world.

'The kitchen's this way,' she said, pointing to a doorway in the opposite wall.

Holding the teapot under one arm, he placed a hand very lightly at her elbow. 'Let's go then.'

'Right.' Feeling just a little breathless, she hurried with him across the hall, making sure she avoided the gaze of anyone else in the room. It would be too bad to be called away now by a teacher or an inquisitive girlfriend.

Once they reached the relative safety of the corridor leading to the kitchen she felt more relaxed. 'Do you have a sister at school here?' she asked him.

'Yes, Annie McKinnon. Sorry, I should have introduced myself.' He switched the teapot to his other arm and offered her his hand. 'My name's Reid. Reid McKinnon.'

'Hi, Reid.' In an effort to suppress her mounting excitement her voice came out rather husky and low. 'Annie's a great kid. I'm Sarah Rossiter by the way.'

'Yes, I know. You're the famous and fabulous School Captain. My little sister idolises you.'

'Annie's a bright spark. I've been coaching her in debating.'

'She's in excellent hands then. I must congratulate you on the speech you gave tonight. It was very, very good.'

'Thank you.' She'd been told this many times this evening, but to her annoyance she felt her cheeks heat. No doubt they were bright pink.

'Such inspiring words of wisdom from one so young.'

She rolled her eyes at him.

He grinned. 'I mean it, Sarah. You were very impressive.'

When they reached the kitchen, Ellen Sparks, the cook, plonked her hands on her hips and scowled at them. 'Do they expect me to make more tea?'

Reid beat Sarah to an answer. 'If you could manage one more pot we'd be extremely grateful.'

He seemed to have the same effect on Ellen that he'd had on Sarah. Instant charm. The cook pouted at him for less than five seconds before her resistance gave way to a cheerful smile. 'No worries, love,' she said, taking the pot. 'It'll be ready in half a tick.'

The kitchen hands scrubbing pots at the sink smirked and giggled.

Just outside the kitchen there was a small walled garden where the cook grew a few herbs. There were gardenia bushes too and white jasmine climbing a rickety trellis and a slatted timber seat where the kitchen staff liked to rest their weary legs and sneak cigarettes when they thought the teachers weren't looking.

'Why don't we park ourselves out here while we're waiting?' Reid suggested.

Sarah could hardly believe that within scant minutes of their meeting she was sit-

ting out here with him—in the romantic
dark, beneath a starry sky and surrounded
by the heady fragrance of jasmine and gar-
denias.

In no time at all she was telling him about
herself—that she was an only child and
came from a cattle property called
Wirralong on the banks of the Burdekin
River not far out of Charters Towers—that
she played guitar, planned to become a primary school teacher and would study at university in Townsville.

And once the tea was ready Reid suggested it made sense to drink it out in the
garden rather than lugging the heavy pot all
the way back into the hall. Sarah hesitated,
momentarily struggling against her usual
tendency to worry about what others might
expect of her. Were her parents or teachers
looking for her?

But another glimpse into Reid's eyes and
she threw caution to the wind. They poured
their cups of tea and helped themselves to

milk, sugar and biscuits from the big kitchen pantry, and took their feast back outside to sit for a little longer in the starlight.

Reid told her about his own boarding school days and the year he'd spent adventuring overseas in Scotland and Europe. And he told her about his family's property, Southern Cross, over to the north in the Star Valley.

The conversation was exceedingly proper and safe and polite, but for Sarah it was incredibly thrilling. It was more than a little flattering to receive what appeared to be sincere and rapt attention from an older, superattractive man.

She feared he might try to crack unfunny jokes that she would have to laugh at, or that he would spoil things by getting sleazy—trying something on—but he didn't. Not once.

'Sarah Rossiter, is that you?'

A shrill, all too familiar voice split the night air behind them.

Startled, Sarah spun around to see the bulky shape of the Deputy Headmistress silhouetted in the light of the kitchen doorway.

Oh, crumbs. She sprang guiltily to her feet. 'Yes, Miss Gresham.'

'Good heavens, girl. What on earth—?' The Deputy gasped and huffed and made a fair imitation of frothing at the mouth. 'What are you *doing* out here?'

Damn. Sarah knew she was about to blacken her exemplary school record. Now, at the eleventh hour.

But, before she could stammer an inadequate reply, Reid stepped forward.

'Miss Gresham, this is my fault. I have to confess to luring Miss Rossiter away from the hall for a well-earned cup of tea.'

'But—but—' the Deputy spluttered.

'And please allow me to congratulate you on your splendid Speech Night. I know you were entirely responsible for organising it. It ran without a hitch.'

Talk about smooth. Within moments Reid had enchanted Miss Gresham the way he'd enchanted Ellen, the cook.

And, starry-eyed, Sarah tumbled heart-first in love with him.

She saw him often over the next four years, while she was at university. They wrote to each other and they got together whenever they could—during her holidays, or whenever Reid found an excuse to get away from Southern Cross and to come down to Townsville.

Every time Sarah saw him she fell a little more heavily in love. And she suspected that Reid was in love with her too. There was plenty of evidence of attraction whenever he kissed her. They didn't make love, but things got pretty steamy at times.

She knew why they hadn't 'gone the whole way'. Reid told her more than once that she was talented and had so much to offer the world that he didn't want to tie her down or hold her back. It was rubbish of course, but it didn't matter how many times she protested, he insisted that she should be free to fully enjoy university life—which included dating other guys.

Reluctantly she accepted that there was some wisdom in this and she went out with several nice enough fellows. It was all very pleasant, but none of the other men ever measured up to Reid.

Then, in her final year, when she came home for the July break, Reid telephoned to say that he was coming over to Wirralong the next day, to visit her.

In a fever of excitement, she dressed in a new pale blue linen shirt and hipster jeans and she stood waiting on the front steps of the homestead, watching for the first cloud of dust that marked the progress of his vehicle along the bush track.

It was a beautiful day—North Queensland at its winter best—a day of high, wide blue skies and air as clear and sparkling as champagne.

When Reid drew close Sarah tore across the lawn and waited at the front gate, then swung it open for him. Through the dusty windscreen she saw the white flash of his smile. *Oh, gosh.* She was so smitten her insides somersaulted with excitement.

He parked beneath a tamarind tree and her heart went crazy as he climbed out. They hadn't seen each other since Easter and now they stood grinning like kids on their first trip to the circus.

Reid seemed taller than she remembered—more gorgeous than ever. He was wearing a dark blue T-shirt and blue jeans. His dark hair probably needed cutting, but she rather liked it curling a little at the ends. He looked so, so handsome. So sexy.

'Hi,' he said, and his smile lit up his eyes, his whole face.

'Hi.'

'I'm not too late, am I? I hope I haven't held up lunch.'

She shook her head. 'Mum and Dad have already eaten, but I've packed a picnic lunch for us to take up the river.'

'A picnic?' He looked surprised—but pleas antly so.

'Are you hungry?'

'Ravenous.'

'I'm afraid it will be a little while before we get there.'

He grinned. 'Cancel the ravenous remark. I can easily wait.'

'Good.' She drew a hasty breath. 'Everything's ready.'

She was rather proud of the way she handled her father's old utility truck through the difficult terrain of Anvil Gully and Retreat Creek. If Reid was impressed by her driving he didn't say so, but he seemed relaxed.

About half an hour later they emerged on top of a high bank on the edge of the Burdekin River.

She felt a little nervous again as they got out and Reid stood beside her. Would he wonder why she'd brought him so far?

Tall, broad-shouldered, strong limbed, Reid seemed part of the rugged wild beauty of the outback. He stood with his thumbs hooked loosely through his belt, looking out at the view of the wide full river and the tall limestone cliffs that guarded it.

From up here it was like looking out from a castle keep. 'What do you think, Reid?'

'It's fantastic. I've never seen this stretch of the river before.'

Satisfied, she turned to get the picnic things from the back of the ute, but he reached out with one hand and caught her waist, pulling her in to him. Her heart thundered wildly as he kissed her. Then he released her and smiled.

'I've missed you, Sarah.'

'Yeah, me too.'

An exquisite shiver trembled through her as he lifted a hand to touch her face, and his eyes feasted on every detail of her features. His thumb brushed her brow, her cheek, her chin.

And then she heard a soft throaty growl and his arms were around her again, hauling her closer, kissing her hungrily now. Backing up against the side of the ute, he pulled her against him so that her feet left the ground and the hard evidence of his desire jutted into her. Electrified, she wound her arms around his neck, returning his kisses as she crushed her eager body against his. A tight coil of longing wound low inside her and her breasts grew tight as heat pooled between her thighs.

Would this be the long awaited day? The day Reid stopped thinking of her as a talented girl and saw that she was a passionate woman, desperately in love?

When he let her go her face was flushed and he smiled self-consciously. 'Hmm, I must have been hungrier than I thought.

Perhaps you'd better show me this lunch of yours.'

They were both sizzling with the heady bliss of being alone together for the first time in ages. Sarah could feel the chemistry arcing between them as they spread her tartan rug in the shade of leafy green quinine trees and Burdekin plums.

She felt excited and breathlessly on edge as she unpacked thick sandwiches filled with marinated roast beef and then a macadamia pie, mandarins and grapes. A bottle of wine and two glasses.

'This is a feast,' Reid declared. 'You've gone to a lot of trouble.'

'Yes.' She smiled. 'I'm all out to impress you.' Then, to cover her embarrassment at being so obvious, she thrust the wine bottle and a corkscrew at him. 'Here, make yourself useful.'

While they picnicked they talked about safe topics like the cattle muster that Reid, his brother Kane and their father had just finished on Southern Cross, about beef prices and the lasting effects of the wet season.

Alone in their remote haven of wilderness, they lay, resting back on their elbows and watching rafts of black ducks, teal and pelicans drift down the river. The water was so clear that even from this high bank they were able to see the darting shadows of black bream swimming.

'You're lucky to have a spot as beautiful as this on your property,' Reid told her.

'I imagine you must have some pretty views on Southern Cross, especially from the ranges looking back across the valley.'

'They're not bad. You should come out to our Cathedral Cave. The view from there is stunning.'

'I'd like that.'

When they'd eaten as much as they could, Sarah began to pack the picnic things away, but before she finished she paused and said somewhat obliquely, 'I like Mirrabrook.'

Surprised, he stared at her.

'I'm thinking of applying for the teaching post there next year.' She knew Reid had been expecting her to go off to teach in one of the big city schools to the south.

He quickly swallowed a last mouthful of pie. 'Are you sure you want to hide yourself away in a little one teacher school in the outback?'

'I'm an outback girl, why shouldn't I want to give something back? Too many young people are leaving the bush for the city.'

'Yes, but—you—you'd have to deal with all those different year levels and there'd be no other teacher to help you find your feet.'

Biting her lip, she looked down at the inch of wine in her glass. Was he trying to put her off? 'It'll be a challenge, but I think I could handle it. I'm going to be a good teacher.'

'I'll just bet you are.'

She downed the wine quickly, set the glass back in the picnic basket, then looked up and saw the dark colour in Reid's face. The strong emotion in his eyes stole her breath.

'What are your chances of getting that post if you requested it?' he asked.

'Nothing's guaranteed, but my good grades should help. Even if they don't, I can't imagine many people will be breaking their necks to teach in Mirrabrook.'

'I don't suppose so.'

Bravely she added, 'But I am.'

'Breaking your neck to be in Mirrabrook?'

She nodded shyly.

'Sarah, it would be wonderful to have you close by.'

Her heart leapt in a quicksilver of joy. 'Well…a girl can hope.'

'And so can a guy,' he said softly.

The look in his eyes made her skin feel too tight for her body. 'Would you—um—like something else to eat?'

'I'd like another taste of that delicious mouth of yours.'

'Come and get it,' she said softly.

A cloud of heat rose through her, making her body flame with outrageous longing. Slowly, Reid leaned towards her, supporting his weight on his hands and knees. His movements were so measured the air seemed to tremble with tension.

In a sensuous daze, Sarah let herself loll backwards till she lay on the rug. She tipped her head back and saw his face register surprise then a slow smile as he lowered his mouth over hers in an upside-down kiss.

She had never imagined anything quite so sexy. Only their mouths touched as they adjusted lips, teeth and tongues to this totally new angle. They kissed in a series of sips and nibbles and sweeping strokes of their tongues. It was fun and yet, oh man, incredibly intimate. Their hunger mounted quickly.

Reid moved from her mouth to sample her chin. With his knees near her head he leaned over her, kissing her throat, then he trailed on, down into the V of her shirt opening.

Sarah's fingers flew to undo her buttons. This was what she had to have. Reid's loving. She was his. Body and soul. She was madly in love with him. No other man would ever mean what he meant to her and she had never given herself this way to anyone else. She wanted to be Reid's. Now. Always.

An astonishing kind of dark wildness overcame her. She needed him. And she felt a sense of panic that perhaps what she wanted most mightn't happen. He might stop too soon.

Perhaps Reid sensed her need, or perhaps, because he'd been waiting as long as she had, he was desperate too. They fought to shed clothes, helped each other to be rid of anything that prevented them from being together skin to skin. Burning skin to burning skin.

Their kisses were fast, hot, hard. Their caresses became greedy, their movements almost savage, their bodies possessed by an urgency that was sky-rocketing out of control.

Then, without warning, Reid pulled away, and he looked upset.

'What?' she whispered, fighting panic. 'What's the matter?'

'This is wrong. It's too wild.'

She felt suddenly cold. 'I—I don't mind.'

'No, Sarah.' His face was flushed. Angry? He was dragging in deep breaths as if struggling for control. 'If we keep on like this I'll hurt you.'

'But I don't want you to stop. I—I want you to make love to me.'

Propped on one elbow beside her, he lifted her dark hair away from her eyes and traced a hand down the side of her face. His eyes were heavy-lidded with desire but he smiled just a little sadly.

He nuzzled her ear. 'Sweetheart, there's no way I want to stop, but let's take this a little easier. We've got all afternoon.' Gently, he pressed his lips to the curve of her throat. 'It'll be even better slow.' He kissed the dip above her collarbone. 'I want this to be special for you. Have you any idea how special you are, Sarah?'

She felt tears spill on to her cheeks. 'They're happy tears,' she hastened to assure him. 'It's just that I've been wanting this for so long.'

'Darling girl, so have I.' He gave a rueful little laugh. 'That's another reason why I want to take it slowly, otherwise it'll be all over before we get properly started.' With the pad of his thumb he wiped the hot path of her tears.

And then he began to kiss her again, slowly, lovingly, while his hands traced her skin with a feather-light touch.

Later, she knew that he'd given her a beautiful gift. Every girl deserved to be made love to for the first time the way Reid made love on that sweet afternoon, with the background hum of bees in nearby wattle and mild winter sunshine spilling through overhead tree branches.

She cried whenever she thought about it.

She was crying now, all these years later, curled up in her chair in the study, clasping the old school programme to her heart.

Oh, Reid, what went wrong?

Tears streamed down her cheeks as she thought of what had followed—that wonderful first year after she'd come to teach in Mirrabrook, when she and Reid were blissfully in love and her world had been perfect.

Throw the programme away. You've got to move on. You've got to forget.

But she couldn't do it. Not yet. She'd throw it away at the end of term when it was time to leave. It would be easier then to get rid of everything in one fell swoop.

Without bothering to dry her damp cheeks, she picked up the drawing pin, stuck it through the hole in the paper and pinned it back on the wall. And felt guilty for being so weak.

CHAPTER THREE

WHEN Annie McKinnon came home to Southern Cross to prepare for her wedding she brought her best friend, Melissa, who would be her chief bridesmaid.

For Reid it was like a breath of fresh air to have his sister home again. He'd been rattling about Southern Cross on his own for too long and he was looking forward to having Annie dashing about, preparing for her wedding.

And he knew he would enjoy having a house full of wedding guests. This homestead was built to take a crowd.

Nevertheless, after months of solitary bachelorhood, it took a little adjusting to get used to having two excited young women chattering non-stop.

'I wonder who wrote this?' Melissa asked one evening soon after they arrived.

Reid looked up from the *Cattlemen's Journal* he was reading. 'Wrote what?'

She held up the latest edition of the *Mirrabrook Star* that had come that day with the mail drop. 'Someone who calls herself Fed Up has sent a Dear Auntie letter to your local paper.'

'What's it about?' asked Annie, who was curled on the sofa with a bridal magazine.

'Listen,' said Melissa. 'I'll read it to you.'

Reid groaned. 'Do you have to?'

'Of course she does, Reid.'

He should have known he'd get no sympathy from Annie. After spending several months in Italy with her fiancé his sister had changed in many ways, but she was as interested in local gossip as she'd ever been. Trying to guess which of the locals had submitted letters to the agony aunt column had always been one of her favourite pastimes.

Now she rolled her eyes at him. 'Don't be a spoilsport.'

Melissa looked from sister to brother, waiting for a decision.

Reid relented. 'Oh, go on then. Read the letter if you must.'

'Okay, this is Fed Up's problem.' Melissa cleared her throat. '"I've been in love with a man for many years, and although I know he once had strong feelings for me, he only offers me friendship now. He's a wonderful man and has been a very good friend, a best friend really, but I can't remain content with friendship alone.

"He never told me why he changed his mind. As far as I know he doesn't have another woman, but do you agree that I'm foolish to hang around year after year hoping he might fall in love with me again?"'

Melissa grinned as she looked up at them. 'Does she really need to ask? What a loser. Anyone you know fit that description?'

Silent seconds later, Melissa frowned. 'Annie, what's the matter?'

Reid didn't hear Annie's reply. He'd jumped to his feet so quickly his chair made a sharp scrape on the polished timber floorboards. But he did hear Annie's worried question. 'Reid, are you okay?'

Of course he wasn't okay. His chest was squeezing so tightly he couldn't breathe. 'I—I just remembered I—I forgot something.' Ignoring his little sister's sweet look of concern, he turned abruptly and strode out of the room and down the passage to the back veranda. Outside, he slammed the back door and sagged back against it, his heart thundering.

Sarah must have written that letter. It couldn't be anyone else. He dragged in a deep breath, trying to calm down. Maybe it wasn't her. She wouldn't want to expose her problem in a public forum, would she?

But it was pointless to speculate. Deep down he knew the writer was Sarah. The

poor girl had been driven to consult an agony aunt and Annie had guessed. After his
pathetic reaction Melissa would probably
guess too. How many others in the district
would guess?

Heaving away from the door, he lurched
across the veranda to the railing and stood
with his hands thrust in his pockets, staring
out at the horse paddock. He should have
found a way to set Sarah free long before
this.

Horrified, he sank on to the back step and
stared out into the silent bush. Clouds
drifted across a new moon, a thin fingernail
of silver, and above the ragged black silhouette of gumtrees the night sky gleamed
a cool gunmetal grey. Down by the creek a
curlew called a long mournful lament.

And Reid wrestled with his despair.

The inevitable day had arrived. The day
he'd been expecting and dreading. The day
Sarah reached the end of her patience. Very
soon she would want to end their friendship

completely. And she had every right to do so. For her own sake, she should have done it long ago.

But, God help him, how could he bear to lose her?

To his horror, he felt his lips tremble. Tears threatened. He shook himself, trying to get a grip, but he felt as lost and wretched now as he had when this nightmare situation had first begun, when he'd been forced to abdicate his role as her lover.

It had damn near killed him to hurt the woman he loved, but in the black days after his father died everything in his world had turned upside-down. It had been the worst, the very worst time of his life—his dark night of the soul.

As he sat in the dark now, Reid wished as he'd wished so many times in the past six years that he could turn to Cob McKinnon for advice. The man had been so much more than simply his father. Reid had looked up to Cob as his hero and he'd loved him as a very special friend. They'd been best mates.

Cob had been a strong man, a tough Scot moulded even tougher by the unforgiving Australian outback. Among the cattlemen in the Star Valley he had been admired as a leader and Reid had grown up idolising him.

No one in his family had realised quite how devastated Reid was when Cob McKinnon died suddenly.

Reid had been away on a muster in the back country and when word came through that his father was gravely ill he'd made a reckless dash for home, riding hard through the night, but he'd been too late.

The worst of it had been that he couldn't give way to the pain that ravaged him; his family had needed him to be strong. His mother had turned to him for help to organize the funeral and to deal with the solicitors and the will.

And Annie and Kane had looked to him for strength too. Although he and Kane were twins, his brother had always deferred to Reid's leadership. And so a huge burden had seemed to fall on him at the very moment he most longed for his father's guidance.

Somehow he had got through it.

But then, things had got worse.

One evening, about a week after his father's funeral, his mother had found him sitting out here on this veranda.

Everything from that night was etched into Reid's brain. He could remember each detail—the oppressive heat that had been building all day; the storm threatening but never quite breaking; the smell of his mother's favourite tea rose oil, cloying on such a hot night; the creak of the old timber floorboards as she crossed the veranda to stand beside him.

'Mind if I join you?' she asked.

'No, of course not.' He jumped up and offered her the more comfortable squatter's chair while he dragged a cane chair closer for himself.

Once she was settled, she said, 'There's something I need to explain to you, Reid.' She paused, as if it was difficult to continue. 'Cob was hoping to talk to you before he died. Poor man, he tried to hang on. He was most anxious to tell you this. But he—he ran out of time.'

Reid thought his father had wanted to explain how their cattle business was to be organised now—whether he and Kane would be entrusted with the running of it, or whether Cob had wanted to appoint a manager from outside the family.

But when Jessie paused again, for an even longer time, he felt a twinge of anxiety. She leaned forward, her elbows resting on her knees and her hands clasped together, her head bowed.

Good Lord, was she praying?

Alarm tightened his guts. 'Mum, are you okay?'

'Not really.' She stared straight ahead. 'Oh heavens, Reid, I'm so sorry. We should have told you this years ago.'

'Told me *what*?'

He stared at her and saw the tension in her profile—her tightly drawn in mouth, her hunched body. 'For God's sake, Mum, what is it?'

'It's—about when you were born.'

The blast of shock hit him in the face as surely as if he'd received a king hit. His heart lurched painfully. Fine hairs rose on the back of his neck. What the hell was this about? His mind raced, trying to drum up possibilities, when Jessie spoke again.

She shifted uneasily. 'I'm sure I've mentioned before that my sister Flora and I both lived in Mirrabrook before I was married. We worked in the bank and we had a little house in town.'

He nodded, wanting to yell at her to stop beating about the bush. *Get on with it. What happened when I was born?*

She sighed. 'As you know, I fell pregnant very soon after I was married.'

'Yeah. With twins. Kane and me.'

'No, darling.' Her voice was excessively careful.

Reid stared at her.

'I wasn't carrying twins.'

Oh, God, Mum, no.

In the moonlight her distressed face gleamed whitely. For the first time in his life he wanted to shake her.

'What are you saying?'

As if she hadn't heard him, or because she couldn't stop now, Jessie hurried on. 'Flora went away to Brisbane soon after I was married and she didn't come back until I was almost ready to give birth. When she did, she brought a little baby with her.'

'No.' Reid collapsed forward, clasping his head in his hands. This was crazy, like some kind of stupid daytime soap opera. He knew what was coming as surely as if he'd written the script. Jerking his head upright again, he dragged in a huge gulping breath. 'You're telling me I was the baby, aren't you?'

'Yes, dear.'

Oh, God. His parents weren't his parents. This was worse than anything he could have imagined. An awful sense of alienation descended. He felt cut off from the woman beside him. He stared at his hands as if he'd never seen them before. Who the hell was he?

How was a man supposed to come to grips with this kind of news. Why now? Why hadn't Cob and Jessie told him this when he was little? Couldn't they have fed him that stuff people dole out to adopted kids about what a special guy he was and how they picked him out because they loved him? At least he would have known all along that he wasn't theirs.

Hell, his whole life had been a lie. As a kid he'd conned himself into thinking he looked like his father. And he and Kane had spent their whole lives thinking they were twins.

The fact that he wasn't even a McKinnon was more than he could bear.

He rounded on Jessie. 'Why did you leave it so damn long to tell me?'

'We—I was worried that you would want to ask too many questions.'

'Sure as hell I have questions. Starting with how did I end up here? With *you*?' He hurled the question at her and the venom injected into *'you'* was intentional. He was angry. Bloody angry. He wanted to lash out.

Her hand fluttered to her mouth and she pressed it against her lips as if she wished she could keep them closed for ever. 'Poor Flora was in a terrible state, Reid, on the verge of a nervous breakdown, and she begged me to take her baby.'

Poor Flora... He didn't want another mother. He most definitely didn't want her to be the Aunt Flora he'd visited briefly in Scotland during his year abroad. His time with her had been uncomfortably brief and strained and he'd come away with the distinct impression that she'd resented his intrusion into her life. 'What was the matter with *poor* Flora?'

Jessie's response was a sharp intake of breath.

Reid glared at her without sympathy. 'You'd better tell me. You've done enough damage keeping these choice bits of news to yourself for so long. No need to spare me now. I want the lot.'

'You won't like it, Reid.'

'Don't let that stop you.'

'Darling, I'm so sorry. I know this is terrible for you. I didn't want to tell you any of this. I—I've chosen the wrong time.'

Damn right she had. They were both too raw with grief to handle this encounter in a civilised manner, but it was too late to stop now.

Reid's jaw clenched. 'What was the matter with my—with Flora? Why did she have to give me away?'

'She'd been raped.'

Raped?

Jessie said the word so quietly he almost didn't hear it above the turmoil of his own thoughts.

But he did hear it. *Raped?* It hit him like a sniper's bullet, scorching through his blood till it found its mark, smack in the centre of his heart. He couldn't think. Just heard that one word screaming over and over and over in his head. *Raped. raped. raped.*

He was the son of a rapist.

A dreadful wailing groan spilled into the night and with a shock he realised the noise was coming from him.

Cursing violently, he sprang out of the chair and stormed down the veranda. He was the son of a rapist. He smashed his fist into a veranda post.

Hell. No wonder Flora hadn't wanted to see him. She must have taken one look at him and seen the image of the man who'd violated her.

'Reid, darling.'

Dimly he was aware of the voice trailing somewhere behind him. Jessie's voice. The mother who wasn't his mother. But what the hell? It didn't matter much who his mother was when he carried the blood of a rapist. He had tainted blood in his veins. In his heart. In his genes. His seed.

Oh, God—

'Sarah.'

Her name broke from his lips on a tortured sob. A vision of her swam before him and he felt suddenly filthy inside. He saw Sarah's lovely oval face framed by her long black hair, saw her warm, full mouth, her light blue eyes, shining with love for him. *For him.* He saw her slender long-limbed body, her divine tip-tilted breasts.

His girl. His gaze dropped to his hands. He'd touched her with these hands. Unworthy hands. He'd done more than that.

For four years he'd been courting her. She was his ideal of womanly perfection. He adored her.

On his last trip to the city, just before his father's death, he'd bought an engagement ring and very soon, when his family weren't so overwhelmed with grief, he was planning to propose to her.

But now… The father he'd loved and buried and grieved for wasn't his father. Had never been his father.

His father was a rapist.

Reid carried bad seed.

How in God's name could he ever marry Sarah now?

No! This had to be a nightmare. 'Tell me this isn't true,' he cried, slamming his hand into the post again.   'Oh, Reid, if only I could.'

Tears blinded him. Angrily he dragged an arm over his face.

'Can I get you something? Would you like a drink, Reid?'

'No, I don't want a drink.'

'Hush, dear, don't wake the others.'

'I want facts,' he hissed. 'I want to know the truth. Where did this happen? Who was this mongrel and where is he now?'

She dabbed at her eyes with a handkerchief. 'I'm afraid I can't tell you much. Flora would never talk about it. It was as if she had blocked it all from her mind. But we've always assumed that the—um—culprit was an itinerant stockman who'd been hanging around town.'

She paused and let out a long sigh. 'He was a nasty type, I'm afraid. He tried twice to break into our cottage. Eventually the Mirrabrook police sergeant ran him out of town, but later he was convicted of raping a woman in Quilpie.'

A wave of nausea rose from Reid's stomach to his mouth. He wiped his lips with the back of his hand. 'Is he still in jail?'

'Apparently he died in prison a couple of years ago.'

He exhaled slowly.

For a long, black stretch of silence they stood, staring out into the night. Then, 'Reid, I don't think we should tell Kane or Annie about this.'

'Of course we shouldn't.'

'Flora didn't want anyone to know.'

'Believe me, I'm not planning to spread the good news.'

'So I can trust you to keep it a secret?'

'Hell, yeah.' He let out a deeply unhappy sigh. More than ever he missed Cob McKinnon. Somehow he was sure this news would have broken over him more easily coming from the old man.

As if reading his mind, Jessie said, 'Darling, Cob loved you. He loved you like—'

'Don't!' Tears came again, breaking up his voice as he shouted at her. 'Don't you dare try to tell me Cob McKinnon loved me like a son. Damn it, I *was* his son.'

The tears coursed down his face as he stumbled down the veranda, away from her, consumed by grief and black-hearted horror.

In the weeks that followed he'd longed to talk about it with Sarah. God knew, it would have been helpful to share the horror with someone, especially if that someone was the woman he loved. But he'd promised Jessie he'd keep quiet and, besides, he knew how Sarah would react.

She would insist that his bad blood didn't matter, that she would love him anyway. But he couldn't ask her to marry him.

Not now that he knew the evil he carried within him. There was no way he would ever permit himself to father a child and he couldn't ask a lovely, healthy, almost certainly fertile young woman to give up her right to motherhood. Sarah loved children.

She was a wonderful teacher and she would be an amazing mother. If he'd asked her to make such a sacrifice, she might have done so willingly in the first flush of young love and then come to resent him after a time.

Which wouldn't be much different from how she felt about him now, he admitted with a soft despairing sigh.

But he'd had another, less noble reason for remaining silent. He'd never been able to bring himself to tell her the truth because he couldn't bear to see the shocked revulsion in her lovely eyes.

But now he knew he'd been selfish. He should have made a cleaner break with her years ago. It would have been kinder to have been cruel then. He should have told her lies, hurt her, said something, *anything* that sent her packing.

Most certainly he should never have come back to her, offering her friendship, and knowing damn well there was every chance she would accept it.

Poor girl. How desperate she must be feeling to have turned to an agony aunt— although he had to admit that on the odd occasion he'd read the column he'd always found her advice surprisingly sane and balanced.

What had she advised Sarah?

Curious suddenly, and feeling calmer now, he took a deep breath and headed back into the house to check the paper.

There was no sign of Annie or Melissa in the lounge room or the kitchen. They'd finished their coffee and had washed their mugs and left them to drain. His half-finished drink had been placed in the microwave.

There was no sign of the newspaper.

Frowning, he scanned the kitchen, searching to see if it had been folded and put somewhere—on a kitchen bench perhaps, or on top of the refrigerator—in the waste paper basket. But it wasn't there.

It wasn't in the lounge room either. He lifted every cushion, went right through the magazine rack and even got down on hands and knees to look under the sofa.

Damn it, Annie had probably wanted to spare him any further embarrassment. No doubt she'd discreetly hidden the paper away, but he needed to know what the agony aunt had said. He had to know what Sarah would do next.

CHAPTER FOUR

THE office of the *Mirrabrook Star* was only four doors from Sarah's school and she sometimes dropped in to visit Ned in the afternoons to share coffee and gossip. A couple of years ago she'd convinced him that he should print a monthly 'school column' in the *Star*, showcasing writing by her pupils—a poem or a little story or a book review.

It had paid off all round. Not only had there been a small but pleasing bump in Ned's sales in the first week of every month, but the lure of being a published writer had worked like a charm on her pupils. Even the most reluctant little wordsmiths now strove to produce their very best work. There was nothing quite so exciting for the children of

Mirrabrook as the glory of seeing their work printed in the *Star*.

Today, as Sarah pushed open the door to the tiny waiting room outside Ned's office, she planned to drop off this month's offering but there was someone inside, talking to Ned.

'I was wondering if I could grab a spare copy of this week's *Star*?' she heard a familiar voice say. 'The newsagents have sold out and Annie burned our copy at home.'

Her heart began a fretful tattoo. The mere sound of Reid's voice sent flashes shooting through her. *Fool.* She mustn't let him affect her this way.

She should leave now. Go home, so she avoided seeing him.

Fat chance. Her feet were glued to the floor.

'Don't tell me Annie's tossed the paper out already?' Ned's voice sounded affronted.

'It was an accident. She put it in the rubbish by mistake.'

Ned chuckled. 'I must say I'm chuffed to think that my little rag is such prime reading that you had to come all the way into town especially, Reid.'

'I—er—had other business.'

Sarah recognised the squeak of Ned's chair. She could picture him moving away from his desk to a bundle of papers on the floor in the corner of the office and extracting one for Reid. 'Here you go, mate. Was there anything in there you were particularly keen to see?'

'Ah—the cattle sale prices.'

Sarah knew he was lying. Her mind whirled. Was Reid hunting down this week's paper because of her letter? She'd been hoping he wouldn't read the column.

After years of handing out advice to others, she hadn't been able to resist putting her own dilemma down on paper. And she'd found the process helpful. It put a little distance between herself and the whole situation with Reid.

At first, she'd had no intention of actually publishing her letter and her reply. But then it occurred to her that it might provide a sense of closure on her life with Reid. With luck, after taking her own good advice, she would be completely free.

But now…

Why was Reid here? Why was he so anxious to read the paper? And what on earth was she doing, waiting here? Any moment now, he would—

'Sarah!'

Oh, help! She came to her senses too late. Reid was already striding out of Ned's office and he looked startled to see her. As upset as she felt.

Her heart took off the way it always did when she saw him. 'R-Reid, fancy meeting you here.'

He seemed flustered and folded the paper in half and tucked it under one arm, as if he hoped she couldn't guess what it was. 'How are you?' he asked and he stared at her anxiously.

Struggling for control, she waved an A4 page. 'I'm fine. I was just dropping off this month's literary masterpiece.'

'Right.' A corner of his mouth quirked as if he tried to smile but couldn't quite manage it. 'Is that something written by one of your pupils?'

'Yes—a poem by Danny Tait.'

He nodded and his eyes gleamed with a puzzling watchfulness.

She considered challenging him about his reasons for coming into town, but Ned's voice boomed through the wall. 'Is that you out there, Sarah?'

Reid stepped out of the office doorway to allow her access.

'Excuse me, Reid.' Grateful for the reprieve, she slipped past him, holding her breath in an unsuccessful effort to prevent the tingling awareness that always pinpricked her skin when she was this close to him.

Ned grinned when he saw her. 'Hi, what literary gem have you brought me this month?'

She handed him the sheet. 'A rather cute little poem.'

He glanced at the page and read the title. *'I wish I had a decent dog.'* Chuckling, he read further and gave a hoot of laughter. 'It's a little ripper. You've sure got a knack with these kids, Sarah. I feel sorry for your replacement. It'll be damn hard to fill your shoes.'

'Ned,' she whispered, cocking her heard towards the anteroom where she feared Reid had lingered. 'That was confidential information.' She hadn't wanted word that she was leaving to leak out until her official transfer came through and she could be quite certain she was actually going.

'Oops, sorry love.'

She glanced towards the doorway and saw the elongated shadow of Reid's head and shoulders.

'Reid won't tell anyone, will you, Reid?' called Ned, raising his voice.

Grim-faced, Reid reappeared in the doorway. 'What won't I tell anyone?'

Oh, good grief, thought Sarah. This was ridiculous.

'Nothing,' she snapped. ''Bye, Ned. Gotta dash.' She hurried out of the office.

Once again Reid had to step out of her way.

''Bye, Reid.'

'Not so fast.' Reid's hand shot out to capture her elbow. His touch electrified her. What was wrong with her? She was supposed to be over this man. Without meeting his gaze, she stood very still and tried to ignore the pressure of his hand on her arm.

'Let's go outside,' he said.

Mutely she allowed him to usher her on to the footpath and then she risked a glance his way and saw stark tension in his eyes and in the tight, hard line of his mouth.

'Are you really leaving town?' he asked her.

'I hope so. I've applied for a transfer.'

He looked away and she saw a small spasm in his cheek as a muscle jerked.

Her vision misted. Damn. She blinked hard. 'It's time I moved on.'

'Yes, I suppose it is.'

This conversation was always going to be hard, but it was even harder on the footpath with people who knew them driving past and waving. 'Would you like to come to my place for a cuppa?' she asked him.

He seemed to be concentrating way off in the distance and took an uncomfortably long time to respond, but then he gave a little shake and turned back to her with a small smile. 'Thanks, I'd appreciate that.'

It was only a short walk to her cottage. Reid seemed to be absorbed with his own thoughts as she opened the door and he followed her through to the kitchen where she boiled water in a jug, scooped tea leaves into a pot and found two mugs. His silence was a blessing really; she wasn't sure how she would handle this conversation.

When the tea was ready they took their mugs out to the little back veranda overlooking the grassy schoolyard and as they settled in deep cane chairs Reid's attention seemed to be captured once again by things in the distance.

Then he said without looking at her, 'You wrote a letter to the agony aunt.'

'Yes.' There seemed to be no point in denying it, although she had no intention of telling him that she'd also written the answer to that letter.

'And what did she advise you? To leave town?'

'Haven't you read the reply?' Sarah glanced back into the house. Through an open window she could see the kitchen table and the folded newspaper he'd left there.

'Not yet. I was about to, but you showed up.' His gaze seemed to be focused on the row of wattle trees at the far end of the schoolyard. 'What did she tell you, Sarah?'

She took a deep breath. 'It was exactly as you've already guessed. She said I should go away.' Emotion filled her throat and she swallowed. 'I think her actual words were—if the situation I described has been dragging on for so many years it's time to do myself and the man in question a favour. I should get out of the picture.'

Had he nodded? She couldn't be sure. But at least he was listening. 'She also said that if this man really loved me, my absence might startle him into action.'

To her horror Reid winced and closed his eyes. Then he stood abruptly and crossed to the veranda rail.

Sarah pressed her lips together and drew another calming deep breath through her nose. 'Don't worry,' she said. 'I know that isn't going to happen.'

He stood sphinx still with his back to her, staring ahead with long distance eyes. 'Anything else?' he asked so faintly she could hardly hear it.

This was so scary. Like tiptoeing through a field of hidden landmines. She and Reid were not making progress. They were still skirting around the edges of a painful conversation that should have been over and done with years ago. Reid was as remote and unreachable as ever and Sarah wasn't sure she was brave enough to continue this terrible charade.

But it was the only way. Distressing as it was, she couldn't back down now. She drank some tea, then set the cup down, rose slowly to her feet and stepped towards the veranda railing.

In the sky high above the schoolyard squawking magpies were mobbing a wedge-etail eagle, chasing it away from their nests and their harsh cries corrupted the peacefulness of the afternoon.

Watching them, Sarah said, 'The agony aunt made one very good point. She said there's a chance that this man is well aware of how I feel but has been too kind to tell me straight out that he's not interested.'

When he didn't respond she wanted to shake him. 'She also suggested the possibility that he might be gay.'

'Gay?' His head jerked sideways and he stared at her, his expression incredulous.

'Yes, well, I didn't take much notice of that.'

Reid grimaced. 'At least this aunt gave you her usual thorough analysis.'

She nodded. 'She wrapped up with a gentle inquiry as to whether the man was my first lover because—because—because it's—' She stopped and bit her lip. 'Because it's always hardest to get over a first love.'

She couldn't tell if the soft sound that broke from him was a groan of impatience or of despair, but she rushed on. 'She said it's time to move on and to start a new life.

Once I'm away from Star Valley I'll make new friends and meet new men. She's confident that in no time I'll be heart whole again.'

A little breeze rushed towards them, rustling through the treetops and skimming over the grassy schoolyard. It played with Sarah's long dark hair and lifted Reid's shirt collar, making it flap against his neck.

'She's given you good advice, hasn't she?'

'Sure,' she said flatly. 'It's the same advice you gave me.'

'Me?' He looked startled.

'You told me once before that I should stretch my wings, remember?'

'Ah, yes.' He nodded. 'When you went to Canada on that teaching exchange.'

'Yes.' Three years ago he'd suggested she should travel and discover the world beyond North Queensland. At the time she'd been terribly upset that he could be so casual about sending her away. Almost to spite Reid, she'd gone away for a whole year.

And in her attempt to forget him she'd flirted with charming young Canadian men and she'd even had one serious boyfriend, but at the end of twelve long months abroad she'd come rushing back to Mirrabrook. Only to discover that nothing had changed, except that her pupils were a year older, or had moved on to high school.

'I should have stayed away then,' she said. 'It was a mistake to come back here.'

He grasped the veranda rail so fiercely his knuckles showed white. His throat worked, and he seemed to be waging an inner battle. He turned and his eyes met hers. At the sight of the bleak desolation in those silvery depths she almost wept.

'I'm so sorry, Sarah.'

Oh, Reid.

His confession broke her heart.

'I know I've let you down badly.' His eyes shimmered with a hint of moisture; his voice was rough with tension. 'You deserved so much more.'

He looked so desolate she wanted to fling her arms around him, but she didn't dare. Nevertheless she felt compelled to console him. 'You can't help it if you—you fell out of love with me.' She was trembling. 'In my head I knew that people fall out of love, but I guess—in my heart I never accepted it.'

Heaven help her, even as she said this she was still foolish enough to hope that Reid might deny it. She still clung to the illusion that her instincts had been right, that he *did* love her.

Now was his chance to be honest.

He turned to her and she saw pain in his eyes and stark anguish twisting his features. 'You understand now, don't you, Sarah? You know that I can't love you?'

Oh, God, there it was. The end of her world. *I can't love you.* Reid had actually said the terrible words.

Her knees almost buckled beneath her. Her eyes filled with hot, embarrassing tears. No, she didn't understand. Was it possible to die? Right then?

The afternoon seemed to grow suddenly dark and she willed the earth to crack open and to swallow her whole. Anything would be better than standing here while Reid McKinnon finally admitted that he did not, could never love her.

How could he do this to her? Why had she set herself up for this ultimate humiliation? How silly to have remained here, dangling on a fragile lifeline of hope for so long.

At this very moment she hated him.

As if to justify his cruelty, Reid said, 'I told you years ago that we shouldn't be more than friends. You know there can't be a relationship, Sarah.'

Struggling for dignity, she felt an urge to fight back. 'Oh, yes, that was what you said, Reid. But how can I be sure you're speaking the truth when I see the way you look at me—when—when y-your guard's down?'

He stood rock-still before her. His face paled and a tremor shuddered through him as if something deep inside had fractured. But when he spoke his voice was ice-cool and certain. 'It's the truth, Sarah. You've been wasting your time here. I'm sorry if you thought I was available.'

Wasting her time? A terrible anger took hold of her. How dared he speak to her this way? Now, after all this time.

She was livid. Furious. She wanted to beat him with her fists and yell at him like a shrew.

But somehow, from some inner strength she hadn't known she had, she managed to rein in her anger and to speak with necessary dignity. '*I* certainly haven't wasted my time. I've had a rewarding and fulfilling career. If anyone's wasted time, Reid McKinnon, it's you.'

Now his eyes were cold. They flickered over her once. 'Perhaps we've said enough.'

Then, while she watched in breathless disbelief, the icy changeling who'd replaced the warm Reid McKinnon she knew strode away from her across the veranda and back through her house. Obtusely, all she could think was that he hadn't thanked her for the tea. Reid was always excessively polite.

She was so distraught she felt mercifully numb. She couldn't bring herself to follow him. She leaned against the railing, listening to the hard ring of his riding boots on the timber floor as he marched through her little house.

It was only after she heard the front door open and then close behind him that she moved. In a daze of horror she flew through the house to the front room. Fool that she was, she still wanted to torture herself by watching through the window as Reid walked away—down the street to his parked utility truck.

But her poor heart shattered when she saw him…still on her front steps, his face buried in his hands…his shoulders hunched and shaking.

Oh, dear heaven. *Oh, dear God.* Surely he wasn't crying?

Her hands flew to cover her mouth. Agonised sobs rose in her throat and she almost ran to the door. But suddenly Reid straightened abruptly. Jumping down the few remaining steps, he hurried down the short path, vaulted her front gate and strode off down the street.

Drowning in a whirlpool of confusion and despair, she watched as he reached his truck, hauled the driver's door open and swung his long body inside. Then the door slammed shut and, without a backward glance, he drove away.

Reid couldn't sleep.

Desolation rampaged through him and gnawed at his insides. Whenever he closed his eyes he saw Sarah.

And he didn't have the strength to hold tormenting thoughts of her at bay. He was powerless to stop the flood of images...

Images that that had never left him...of Sarah in his arms...in his bed. She haunted him with maddening, teasing fantasies. He could remember every intimate detail of the precious days and nights they'd shared in that halcyon time before Jessie McKinnon's shocking revelations.

Now he burned as memories stormed him. He needed to taste Sarah's sweet pink mouth again, needed to run his tongue over that sexy, pouting lower lip of hers. He ached with the memory of her slender body. He longed to feel the weight of her breasts in his hands, to crush her lush and lovely curves beneath him, to lose himself in her.

Instead, she was lost to him...because of the sins of his father.

And she'd been such an innocent, trusting girl when they had met.

He'd had no warning that at the ripe age of twenty-five his world would be rocked by a schoolgirl, but from the moment Sarah had walked on to that Speech Night stage to deliver her School Captain's address she'd captured his rapt attention.

He'd been electrified. His boredom had vanished in an instant. He'd stopped leafing through the programme and watched her, transfixed.

Afterwards, he'd tried to pinpoint exactly what had triggered that first emotional wallop that deprived him of oxygen. He'd never experienced such a reaction to a girl.

The way she'd looked had been part of it—tall and slender with sleek black hair and dancing light blue eyes and the most kissable mouth he'd ever seen.

But right from the first he'd detected her inner radiance too, a natural confidence that seemed to shine from within when she smiled out at her audience.

And then she'd begun her speech and his interest in how she'd looked had been eclipsed by his fascination with her voice and her message.

He could still remember parts of that speech, how she'd issued a word of warning to her fellow students who, like her, were about to head off into the world full of bright hope.

'I don't pretend to be wise,' she'd told them. 'But one thing I've learned during the seventeen years I've been on this planet is that we must expect pitfalls along the way. There will be times when our goals seem unreachable.'

Oh, God, how prophetic her words had been.

What had he done to that bright young woman? He should never have given in to his urge to meet her that night. He should have let her go then.

Instead he'd become her major pitfall.

Instead of letting her march away from him, instead of sending her out into the world where she could make her mark and forge a brilliant career, he'd lured her into the outback with promises he'd never been able to keep.

At the time she'd reminded her fellow schoolgirls of how gutsy they'd been when they were very young—when they were first learning to walk.

'If we could get up, dust ourselves off and start again when we were only one year old, we will be able to do it now as we stumble our way through the challenges of adulthood,' she'd told them.

But he'd given the poor woman one stumbling block too many.

With an angry cry he leapt from the bed and stood staring through the window into the dark, brooding, silent bush. There was so much about Sarah that he would miss. Once she left Mirrabrook all contact would be cut off. He would lose touch with her kind and courageous heart, her quick and clever mind, her calm and wise spirit.

He damn near worshipped the woman.

And today he'd looked into her soft blue eyes and told her what he should have told her years ago, that he could never love her.

But the lie had cost him dearly. Damn it, he might never sleep again.

He had to remember that his task now was to focus on Sarah's happiness. Once she left she would be free of him. She would be able to marry and have a child of her own. She would be the perfect mother— of a child he could never father.

Enough! He began to prowl restlessly through the midnight-dark homestead. Clouds covered the moon, but the house was so familiar to him that he could find his way easily in the inky blackness. His bare feet made no sound.

When he reached the kitchen he decided against using the electric light which might wake Annie and Melissa and found the fat orange candle that the girls had left sitting in a saucer on the table. He lit it and by its gentle light he made a cup of tea.

According to Annie, the aroma of citrus and vanilla wafting from the candle was supposed to be calming. Not tonight. In his T-shirt and boxer shorts, he paced the room, taking fretful gulps of tea. And he told himself for the thousandth time that he'd done the right thing today. It had been vital to tell Sarah that he couldn't love her. He had to help her to make that absolute break.

Once she got over her hurt she would be able to move on, to make a new life. He had absolutely no right to hold her back from that life. She deserved and needed a good and steady man, a man who would marry her and make her happy and become the father of her children.

A groan escaped him. How could he bear it? When she left he would still be here, forever missing her.

He'd thought he'd come to terms with a passionless existence and an essentially lonely life, but until now Sarah had always been there in the background.

Now he saw a picture of himself growing old here. Alone. Hell, he was only in his mid thirties, so he had a long time to go...living out the empty decades through his forties and fifties and sixties...watching Kane and Charity and Annie and Theo all happily married and raising families.

Just yesterday a jubilant Kane had rung from Lacey Downs with the news that he and Charity were expecting their first baby.

Another groan burst from him and he knew he had to stop thinking this way, had to get a grip. He hated feeling maudlin; he had no time for people who moped around feeling sorry for themselves, but right now he couldn't get his head past the scary desolation and emptiness inside him.

'I thought I heard noises out here.'

Reid whirled around to find Annie coming into the room, wearing amazing lime silk pyjamas.

She peered at him in the subdued light. 'Are you okay, Reid?'

'Yeah, I'm fine.'

'You don't look fine.' Flopping on to a kitchen chair, she ran her hands through her sleep-tumbled hair, then hooked one foot up on the chair and hugged her knee. By candlelight she appeared impossibly young, like the little sister he used to tease.

'You looked dreadful at dinner this evening,' she said.

When he shrugged she smiled at him. 'This conversation sounds like a reversal of the one you had with me last summer when I was breaking my heart over Theo.'

'Course it's not. I don't have a broken heart. Don't get carried away, Annie. I don't need counselling from my baby sister.'

'But you can't pretend that you're not upset.'

He grimaced. 'I'm fine. Forget it and go back to bed. You're going to be a bride in a few weeks' time and you need your beauty sleep.'

Ignoring this she said, 'I know that agony aunt letter in yesterday's paper was from Sarah Rossiter.'

At the sound of Sarah's name he stiffened. 'What if it was?'

'This man she talked about. He was you, wasn't he?'

Without answering he resumed pacing.

'I know it's upsetting you, Reid. You were so mad at me for burning that paper and you went tearing off into town.'

'The two things aren't connected. You're jumping to conclusions.'

'I don't think so, big brother.' Annie's voice was soft, laced with concern. 'It's always been obvious that there was something between you and Sarah. You've pretended to be "just friends" but, well—now it's clear that Sarah has wanted a whole lot more and I—I can't help thinking you do too.'

He stopped pacing to glare at her. 'Give it a miss, Annie.'

'I'm not sure that I should give it a miss. Actually I think I've been overlooking too much. Both Kane and I have been so caught up with ourselves we haven't been looking after you.'

He slammed the mug down on the kitchen bench. 'I don't need looking after. I don't want anyone fussing over me.'

'But Reid, I know something's wrong.' Annie threw up her hands in a melodramatic gesture of despair. 'This situation feels like a tragedy to me.'

Her words cut into him like a knife thrust. She was right. This was a flaming tragedy. Nevertheless, he leaned back against a cupboard and crossed his arms over his chest with a deliberately casual air. 'You're getting fanciful, kiddo. Theo's been taking you to too many Italian operas.'

Jumping out of the chair, she hurried around the table and slipped her arms around his waist. His throat grew tight as her glossy blonde hair brushed his cheek and she pressed her face into his shoulder. Damn it, he didn't want displays of affection. He was having enough trouble handling his own emotions.

She said, 'This is a tragedy because Sarah's a beautiful person and you're an amazingly wonderful man and the two of you are made for each other.'

'For God's sake, Annie, leave it alone.' Reid jerked away sharply, breaking free of her embrace. 'Give me some space. Just focus on your wedding.' When she opened her mouth to protest, he silenced her with a raised hand. 'You really do jump in at times when you're not wanted, little sister. And *this* is one of those times.'

Venting his despair with a savage sweep of his hand, he injected his words with uncharacteristic menace. 'I don't want you sounding off about this ever again.'

She gasped. 'Sounding off?'

He was already storming out of the room. Over his shoulder he caught a glimpse of Annie's white, stunned face. In the candle-light her eyes were dark pools of hurt shock.

And wasn't that just *great*. Now he'd bru-tally wounded another woman he loved.

CHAPTER FIVE

'WHAT do you think, Sarah?'

Annie lifted a rose-pink gown from folds of tissue paper and held it up for inspection. She'd bought her wedding dress and the dresses for the bridesmaids from a bridal shop in Rome and now, on Saturday afternoon, Sarah had come out to Southern Cross for a fitting.

'It's a lovely silk and a beautiful colour.'

'I chose deep pink for you to go with your gorgeous black hair,' said Annie. 'Mel's wearing a—'

'A medium shade of pink to go with my medium brown hair,' cut in Melissa with a self-conscious grin.

Annie waggled a finger at her friend. 'It's called blush and it suits you beautifully and you know it, Melissa Browne.'

Sarah looked at Melissa's dress, which was hanging on the front of Annie's wardrobe. 'It looks lovely too.'

'My other bridesmaid, Victoria, has redgold hair, so she'll be wearing the palest of pale pinks,' Annie added.

Sarah smiled. 'We'll look like a bouquet.'

'I'll call you my rosebuds,' Annie said with a laugh. Then she grew impatient. 'Hurry up and try this on, Sar, I can't wait to see you in it.'

Sarah obliged, slipping out of her skirt and top and lifting her arms while Annie guided the silken gown up and over her. 'If it doesn't fit perfectly, Vera Jones is a whiz with alterations.'

But even before Sarah looked into Annie's bedroom mirror she knew there would be no need to bother Vera Jones. As soon as the tiny buttons were closed she could sense that the dress fitted her like a dream.

'Oh, boy! Oh, wow! Sarah, you look absolutely gorgeous.'

Sarah turned to look in the full-length mirror and her breath caught with surprise as she saw her reflection. With the special flair that comes with Italian design, the neckline of the slim-fitting sleeveless gown was cut into a flattering low cowl at the front, with a deep V at the back. The dark rose of the silk was the perfect foil for her dark hair and pale skin.

'All my bridesmaids are going to look so lovely,' said Annie, her eyes dancing with excitement.

'And Sarah and Reid are both tall and dark. You'll look fantastic together,' added Melissa.

Sarah and Reid?

Frozen with shock, Sarah watched her reflection in horror as a tide of colour, as deep pink as her dress, rose from her chest to her throat and into her cheeks. She turned to Melissa. 'What did you say?'

In the mirror she saw Annie behind her, madly shaking her head and frowning a warning to Melissa.

'Why would I be together with Reid?' Sarah asked.

Both girls looked suspiciously sheepish.

She challenged Annie. 'My partner for the wedding will be one of the groomsmen, won't he? One of Theo's friends. Reid will be giving you away.'

Annie looked anxious and chewed her lip.

Sarah's heart began to pound. 'Annie?'

'Kane's going to give me away,' she said. 'Because Theo has asked Reid to be a groomsman.'

This time Sarah could feel herself going pale. She glanced towards the mirror. Yes, sure enough, at the thought of walking down the aisle with Reid her colour was draining quickly. 'I—I don't understand.' What perverse kind of irony was this? 'How can Reid be a groomsman? I thought Theo would ask his friends from—from Brisbane.'

'Yes, Theo has asked two friends from Brisbane. One of them will be the best man and he'll be Mel's partner, but Theo's asked Reid to be a groomsman too. You see, Theo came out to Southern Cross at the end of last year and he and Reid hit it off. The two of them have become quite good friends.' Annie smiled cautiously. 'Reid was kind of instrumental in getting us together.'

'I—I see.'

Annie let out a short sigh. 'Sarah, I could do a swap, I guess, but the other groomsman is rather short, like Victoria, and it might look a little odd if I teamed him with you.'

Melissa eyed both Annie and Sarah with a look of complete puzzlement. 'I apologise in advance for being really thick, but why wouldn't you want Annie's brother as a partner? I think he's a darling. Very hot looking too.'

Sarah drew a deep breath. 'Of course he's nice.' She stopped and struggled to think how she could justify her reaction, but Annie leapt to her aid.

'Mel, life in the bush might look simple but things can get just as complicated here as they do in the office in Brisbane.'

Mel grimaced. 'Sorry if I've put my foot in it.'

'I'm the one who should be apologising,' protested Sarah, feeling sorry for the poor girl.

'Maybe I should make myself useful with afternoon tea,' Mel suggested tactfully.

Annie threw an arm around her friend's shoulders. 'Thanks, hon. Why don't you go and set the glasses and the jug and everything out on the cane table on the veranda? We'll be out in a minute.'

'Yes, of course.

'I've embarrassed your friend,' Sarah said as Melissa hurried out of the room.

'Don't worry about Mel. I'll square things with her. I'm more worried about you, Sarah.'

'I'm all right really. It's just that I was a bit gobsmacked to hear that Reid's in the wedding party. I had no idea he'd met your Theo.' She turned back to the mirror and tried to change the direction of her thoughts as she eyed her reflection thoughtfully. 'You've done well to find a ready-made dress that fits so beautifully.'

'I'm lucky you have such a well-proportioned figure.'

'Mmm. Help me out of this again, Annie.'

As Annie carefully eased the dress back over Sarah's head she said, 'I saw your letter to the agony aunt.'

Sarah wasn't surprised that Annie had guessed. Just the same, mention of the letter caused a queer little twist in her heart. She was quiet till the dress had been hung safely on a padded satin hanger then she said,

'Don't start worrying about that letter, Annie. Reid and I have discussed it. Everything's sorted out.'

Annie eyed her doubtfully. 'Are you sure about that?'

'Absolutely.' Sarah pulled her T-shirt back over her head and reached for her denim skirt. 'I'm going away. I've applied for a transfer and I'm expecting to hear any day that I've been posted to a school on the coast.'

'Yes, I know.'

'Who told you?'

'Rhonda at the Post Office.'

Sarah rolled her eyes. 'Great. That means the whole district knows I'm going.'

'That's country towns for you.'

'I wonder how she found out? Probably from Ned, the editor of the *Star*.'

Sighing, Annie shrugged. 'Sarah, I'm not so sure that you and Reid have everything sorted out. I'm worried about my big brother.'

Sarah's heart seemed to trip and her fingers fumbled with the button on the waistband of her skirt. 'Why? What's wrong with him?'

For a moment Annie didn't answer. She sank down on to the edge of her bed and patted the space beside her. 'Sit down for a minute.'

Sarah remained standing. 'Annie, I don't think I can cope with a deep and meaningful about this.'

Annie looked even more worried. 'Are things that painful?'

'They're not too chipper.' Sarah blinked. 'But everything will be fine once I'm out of Star Valley.'

'I hope I haven't created problems for you by teaming you with Reid, Sarah. I had it all planned before—before I saw the letter in the *Star*.'

'Does he know I'm going to be his partner?'

Annie nodded.

'And he doesn't mind?'

She shrugged. 'He *says* he's cool.'

'Then everything's okay, isn't it?' Sarah forced a swift smile then bit her lip when she saw the doubt in Annie's eyes. 'Why do you think there's something the matter with Reid?'

'I was hoping you might be able to give me a clue.'

Sarah lifted her hands in a gesture of helplessness. 'I don't know, Annie. I really don't.'

Giving in, she dropped on to the bed beside Annie. 'Reid told me that he doesn't love me. He said that we have no future but, fool that I am, I still can't bring myself to believe him.'

With the knuckle of her little finger she wiped a tear from the corner of her eye. 'It's ridiculous to still be hoping after all this time. I must be a total basket case, because even though Reid looked me in the eye and said that he doesn't love me I still have this feeling that he's hiding something.'

'So do I.'

Sarah stared at her. 'Do you? Really?'

Annie took time to think about her answer. 'I reckon something happened to Reid back around the time that our father died. Remember how he became all withdrawn and brooding? I'm sure it was more than grief for Dad.'

'Yes, that was about the same time that everything went wrong between us.'

Annie nodded. She sat very still as if lost in thought, then gave her friend a swift hug. 'Don't lose heart, Sarah. You know, I have a feeling that my mother might hold the answer to this problem.'

'Your mother?'

'She's been living in Scotland since our father died, but she's coming out for the wedding. She'll be here next week and—'

She broke off as the clomp of hurried footsteps rang through the house. Reid charged into the room and came to an abrupt halt when he saw Sarah sitting on Annie's bed.

Both girls leapt to their feet.

'What's the matter?' Annie asked him.

For a moment he looked dazed as he stared at Sarah. Then he gave a little shake as if to gather his wits. 'I—I've just had word from Orion Station that little Danny Tait's gone missing.'

'Danny?' cried Sarah. 'Where is he missing?'

'Is he one of your pupils?' asked Annie.

'Yes.'

'They think he's still somewhere on his family's property,' said Reid. 'Apparently he took off early this morning before breakfast and he hasn't been seen since.'

Sarah glanced at her watch. It was three-thirty in the afternoon. Danny had been missing for nearly ten hours and Orion Station was almost as big as Southern

Cross—thousands of hectares of rugged bush.

'Do you know if he took food or water with him?'

Reid shook his head. 'His mother isn't sure. There's a chance he didn't. As far as Diane can tell there are no water bottles missing. Danny certainly hasn't had a proper meal today.'

'Diane will be beside herself.' Sarah frowned. 'I guess the family have already been searching for him.'

'Yeah. For most of the day. Now they've called the police sergeant and he's sending out a call for local volunteers.'

'Right.' Sarah looked towards Annie. 'I'll have to go, Annie. Next to his parents I probably know Danny best of anyone in the district. He's a very highly strung kid. He has Asperger's syndrome and he could be frightened by strangers, so the more searchers who know him the better.'

'Goodness. Poor kid.'

'I'm heading off now,' Reid told her.

Sarah didn't hesitate. 'I'll come with you.'

When he nodded she ignored the *frisson* that shimmied through her.

'Should I come?' asked Annie.

'No.' Reid was decisive. 'Theo would never forgive me if I let you go scrambling about in the scrub. You don't want to turn up for your wedding covered in scratches. Besides, you should stay here with your city girlfriend.'

Sarah was already thinking ahead. 'We should take some water and warm clothes in case the search extends into the night.'

'Sarah, you might want to borrow a pair of my jeans and a jacket,' Annie volunteered. She eyed Sarah's sandals. 'Try my boots for size too.'

'I'll be packing the other things we need into the ute.' Reid's eyes were steady as they rested on Sarah. 'I'll park the ute around the front of the house. See you there in five.'

CHAPTER SIX

IN LESS than five minutes Sarah and Reid were heading away from Southern Cross, bouncing down the dusty dirt track that led across the Star Valley to Orion Station. Reid knew the road well and was able to dodge ruts and potholes as he drove quickly and expertly. At first he didn't speak and Sarah sat beside him quietly contemplating the bizarre twists of fate that seemed to be throwing her into contact with this man despite her best efforts to leave and forget him.

His voice broke into her thoughts. 'I hate to think of a little kid lost in this rough country. There's so much thick scrub and rocky gullies.'

She looked out at the rugged bushland rushing past them, at the rocky ground, the clumps of tall spear grass and the endless trees—ironbarks, bloodwoods, quinine and brigalow, and every so often silver-leafed wattles. It would be so easy for a small boy to disappear amongst them and never be found.

There were so many awful things that might have happened to Danny. He could have been bitten by a snake, or he might have fallen down a gully and injured himself. Perhaps he hadn't been able to find water and was dehydrated and disoriented.

She turned to Reid. 'A child lost in the bush is an outback mother's worst nightmare.'

He nodded grimly. 'I hope this new police sergeant's got what it takes to coordinate a proper search.'

'Heath Drayton? Why shouldn't he be good at his job?'

'He's only been in Mirrabrook a month or so. He's young and green and fresh from the city; he mightn't know how to cope in the bush.'

'He seems very switched on to me.'

'Switched on to you?' His mouth thinned into a grimacing smile. 'Well, yes, he would, wouldn't he?'

'What do you mean?'

'A young copper, all bright and bushy-tailed from the big smoke, would take a shine to a pretty young country school-teacher.'

Good heavens. Was this a touch of jealousy from the man who'd so decisively cast her aside? 'Hmm… I'll have to make sure I smile at him very nicely then, won't I?'

She wasn't surprised when Reid didn't reply. But after a stretch of silence he asked, 'What can you tell me about Danny Tait? I haven't had much to do with him since he was an ankle biter. You said he has some kind of problem.'

'He has Asperger's syndrome, which means he's slightly autistic.'

He frowned. 'How does that affect his behaviour?'

'On the surface he's perfectly normal. Danny's quite bright, actually. He's an obsessive reader and he writes some wonderful little poems, but his social skills are poor. In the classroom he comes across as a little odd. He makes inappropriate remarks at times and he's hopeless at joining in group activities. He's not very popular with the other students, poor lamb.'

After a bit she added, 'When he's older he'll probably get along fine in Internet chat rooms.'

'But is he the type of kid who'd take off into the bush?'

'I suppose he might. He's a loner. He might have wandered off looking for a quiet place to read. Or perhaps something upset him. He probably wouldn't give any thought to the anguish he'd cause his parents.'

Sarah thought about the boy's behaviour over the past week. 'I didn't notice anything unusual about Danny at school. But I must say I'm surprised he's skipped his meals. He's a great stickler for routine, doesn't like change, or anything that disrupts the pattern of his day.'

Reid sent her a quick smile. 'Don't worry too much. With luck they'll have found him before we get to Orion.'

She returned his smile and, despite her fears for Danny, she thought how good it was to be having a straightforward conversation with Reid. It made a refreshing change to put their personal issues aside for once and to join forces to tackle someone else's problem.

Staring ahead, Reid said, 'Danny's been lucky to have you as his teacher.' Then he directed another glance her way. 'You know, I don't think I've ever heard you say a bad word about any one of those kids you teach.'

'Oh, there are plenty of times when they make me mad.' She couldn't help adding,

'You don't know me as well as you think you do.'

Reid flinched and kept his eyes strictly on the road, his face hard. They were approaching a rattling cattle grid bridge which required extra concentration—a good excuse to lapse back into silence.

Perhaps that was just as well, she decided. If they weren't discussing Danny there weren't a lot of safe topics left for them.

They didn't talk again till they reached the Taits' property. A good collection of people had already arrived. People from the township of Mirrabrook and from the surrounding properties had dropped what they were doing and rushed to join in the search.

Heath Drayton, the police sergeant, had set up a command centre on the homestead's front veranda. Maps were spread on one end of a long trestle table and there was a pile of CB radios on the other.

'I've had one chopper diverted from a muster to do an air search,' Heath explained to the group. 'There's a party including Danny's parents out on horseback, working in pairs, and there are also three trail bikes out there. But the quicker we can cover the ground the better chance we have of finding this little bloke.'

With a pencil the sergeant drew a circle on the map to define the search.

He looked directly at Reid. 'I'd like you to have a closer look at this area near the cattle yards down towards the creek, Reid. Just before you got here I picked up footprints. They could be Danny's and I've been told you're our best bet for tracking him until I can get an Aboriginal tracker down from Greenvale.'

Reid nodded thoughtfully. 'I can't promise I'll be able to find tracks if they leave the sandy country and move on to rocky ground.'

'Give it your best shot.' Heath signalled for the rest of the volunteer searchers to come closer. Sarah had been waylaid by some of the other women, but now she joined Reid as everyone formed a semi-circle in front of Heath.

'Okay, folks, listen up. We can't afford to wait any longer. You've all been given an area to cover. Danny's mother is pretty sure he's wearing a red T-shirt, which is handy because it should show up easily. Now, as you comb the area you've been allocated I want you to pause frequently to look ahead, to the back and from side to side, and call out Danny's name.'

Reid turned to Sarah and muttered out of the side of his mouth. 'This young copper's shaping up pretty well.'

She smiled wryly. 'Maybe he's not such a greenhorn after all?'

'One last thing,' said the sergeant. 'If you find any of the boy's belongings don't touch them or move them. Just note the position carefully and then report it. We want to leave it in place and not disturb any tracks.'

'You've been teamed with me,' Reid told Sarah and although his mouth was grim there was the faintest hint of a smile in his eyes.

Sarah nodded calmly enough, but she pulled the hat she'd borrowed from Annie lower over her face to shield her eyes from his. This was the way it always was. Their friends and the broader community had never stopped thinking of Reid and Sarah as partners. They didn't seem to notice that there was nothing there, that the relationship was an empty shell.

Well, the people of the Star Valley were in for a shock when the Reid 'n Sarah charade was exposed.

But she couldn't think about that now. As they set off she thanked heaven that she had something definite to focus on instead of the crazy tug of distressing attraction she always felt when she was with this man.

The section of country they were given began with a relatively flat sweep of semi-open bushland heading down to the creek. Reid picked up the small footprints quite easily and while they kept to sandy ground Sarah found that she could follow them too.

But as Reid continued at a brisk pace the trail became less and less visible to Sarah and it disappeared completely when they reached the grassy, rock-strewn creek bank.

'Can you really still see tracks here?' she asked him.

He smiled. 'I'm not actually looking for a track now. I'm looking ahead to see what's been disturbed.'

She peered at the ground and shook her head. 'Your eyes must be a jolly sight better than mine.'

'It's not so much a matter of superior eyesight. You've just got to know what to look for. Things like grass pushed aside, or overturned rocks or displaced pebbles.'

'Who taught you how to do this?'

'My father. He learned it from Mick Wungundin, an Aboriginal stockman who worked on Southern Cross years ago.' He grinned. 'The way Dad told it, Mick could track a fish through water.'

Sarah laughed.

'But don't expect anything like that from me.'

It wasn't too much longer before he stopped. With his hands resting lightly on his hips he looked around him, his eyes narrowed against the low angled glare of the afternoon sun and he surveyed the country with a thoughtful frown.

Sarah followed his gaze, not sure what he was looking for. She thought how lovely the bush was at this time of day when the afternoon sun turned the pink feathery tops of the grasses into a shimmering sea of colour.

'It's my guess that if Danny took off because he's upset, he probably followed this creek,' said Reid. 'There's no real reason for him to try to cut across country unless he's trying to get somewhere specific.'

'So we'll push on along here?'

'Actually, I think the best thing we can do is go back and get the four-wheel drive and follow this creek out for about ten kilometres or so. I don't think a little bloke would have gone much further than that.'

She nodded. It was a sensible decision given that there wasn't much daylight left. Even as they turned back for the homestead to collect the ute, the sun was beginning its descent towards the western rim.

The quiet afternoon was pierced by the raucous cries of sulphur crested cockatoos, chasing each other into the ti-trees on the far side of the creek. Reid radioed their change of plan through to Heath Drayton.

'Sounds like a good idea,' Heath agreed. 'Just make sure you keep in touch.'

'Sure.'

He was about to disconnect when Heath said, 'Reid, if you don't find Danny in the next hour or so, I'd like you to stay out there tonight. Set up a campfire that Danny might see.'

Hearing this, Sarah bit her lip. She hadn't allowed her mind to consider the possibility that she might need to spend this night alone in the bush with Reid. Could her nerves stand the strain?

Her eyes sought his and to her dismay he was watching her with a carefully cool, almost impersonal air of detachment.

Heath's voice crackled into the awkward silence. 'Is that a problem?'

'Is it a problem, Sarah?' Reid asked quietly.

'Sarah can stay back at the homestead if she wishes,' Heath added.

Reid's face was a blank mask. 'You don't have to stay with me.'

His lack of emotion hurt her more than she could bear, but in an act of sudden defiance she rushed to assure him, 'No, of course it's not a problem. I need to be out here looking for Danny tonight. He knows me and trusts me.'

Reid nodded. 'You won't be too uncomfortable. There are two swags in the back of the ute and I've plenty of water.'

Surely he must know it wasn't the lack of physical comfort that bothered her. 'I'll be fine,' she said.

He spoke into the radio again. 'Heath, we can do the night stint.'

'Great. Make sure you grab a Thermos of tea and some packets of sandwiches from the women at the homestead.'

'Will do.'

'And, when you set up camp, try to have plenty of light around you. It might attract Danny in.'

After picking up the ute and food supplies, they had only travelled a short distance before Reid slowed the truck and turned to Sarah. 'Are you sure you wouldn't rather stay back at the homestead?'

She sighed. 'I have to come. Especially now.'

He frowned. 'Why especially now? What's happened?'

'I've just heard that I'm responsible for what's happened to Danny.'

'For the kid's disappearance?'

'Yes.'

'How on earth could it be your fault?'

'Apparently he's upset because he's heard that I'm leaving.'

A dark red tinge stained his cheekbones. 'Who told you that?'

'Linda Hill, Danny's aunt. She told me just now when I went inside to get our sandwiches.'

Reid cursed softly. 'Why can't people mind their own bloody business?'

The intensity of his reaction surprised her. 'I'm sure it's true. Danny hates change. It's not that he's particularly attached to me. Kids with Asperger's don't often form close attachments, but he would be upset about getting a new teacher because he'd hate the disruption.'

Reid gritted his teeth as he depressed the accelerator and edged the vehicle forward again. 'Who told Danny you were leaving? It's not public knowledge, is it?'

'Apparently the bus driver told all the kids on the way home from school yesterday afternoon.'

'The *bus* driver?' Reid's fist thumped the steering wheel. 'Every man and his dog are in on this.'

She sighed. 'I know.'

'I'm surprised you've been so public about our personal affairs.'

Sarah gasped, astonished that Reid still saw himself as part of her life—part of her problem. 'I haven't been broadcasting the fact that I'm leaving. Be fair, Reid. You know what gossip's like around here. Everyone's private affairs become public property. It's impossible to keep anything a secret.'

'No, it's not.' He snapped this so fiercely he might have bitten her head off.

Shocked, Sarah struggled for breath and her chest squeezed tight as she stared at him. This was the very first time Reid had admitted something that deep in her bones she'd suspected for a long time. 'Are you telling me you've been keeping secrets?'

His knuckles turned white as he gripped the steering wheel. 'I was speaking hypothetically.'

Rubbish. He'd been speaking the truth. But she could sense that already he regretted his mistake. Just the same, his admission had provided a possible clue to his perplexing behaviour. Was there a dark secret in his life that prevented him from loving her?

She sighed. If there was a secret he hadn't been able to share it with her and what did that say about the depth of their relationship? Surely if Reid had ever loved her he would turn to her in times of trouble, not away from her?

His voice broke into her wretched thoughts. 'Do you know when you'll be leaving Mirrabrook?'

'No.' She lifted her shoulders in an exaggerated shrug. 'The transfer hasn't come through yet. That's why these rumours are so annoying. There's nothing official and unless I get something on paper I won't be going anywhere.'

He shot a quick glance in her direction and she fancied she saw a flicker of hope in his eyes, but it was so fleeting she was probably mistaken. He jerked his gaze back to the front. Too quickly. His throat worked rapidly as if he were struggling with inner turmoil.

Her stomach plunged. This night alone in the bush was going to be difficult for both of them.

The journey was rough and as they bounced and bashed their way through the scrub Sarah kept her eyes peeled for a flash of colour or anything different, but the task was made more difficult by the diminished light and the deep shadows that striped the undergrowth.

Every hundred metres or so they stopped to look around carefully and to get out of the ute to call Danny's name. But the only response was the hushed silence of the bush and the occasional bird call.

They didn't find him before it grew dark, but they pushed on, stopping to toot the horn and to call out. Sarah didn't want to give up, but eventually, when they reached a clearing, Reid stopped the vehicle. 'I don't think it's worth going much further,' he said.

Feeling more than a little dejected, they built a campfire and sat on their rolled out swags drinking tea from the Thermos. The red firelight lit up their faces and the trunks and branches of the trees around them, but beyond that small circle of light the bush was pitch black.

'I wonder if Danny's afraid of the dark,' mused Reid.

Sarah frowned. 'I'm not sure. I've taught all the children how to make fires and I've told them to always carry a pocket knife, matches and water when they're in the bush, but he may have been too upset to think of things like that.'

They lapsed back into silence and Sarah tried not to think too much about Danny, alone out there in the black, lonely scrub. But when she stopped thinking about the little lost boy her thoughts turned to her conversation in Annie's bedroom this afternoon—what Annie had said about Reid's reaction to his father's death—that something more than grief had taken hold of Reid.

It wasn't sensible to think about that either, but she couldn't help herself. It might hold the clue to the secret he'd hinted at—to her years of heartbreak.

What could have happened? She'd never really believed that grief alone could have caused Reid to fall out of love with her. It was such a difficult question to put to a man, but she should have pushed him for a proper answer years ago, when he'd first begun to distance himself from her.

Tipping her head back, she stared up at the sky. In the patch of inky heaven directly above their clearing, the Milky Way meandered like a river of stardust. She sighed as she dropped her gaze again and stared into the fire.

There was something very mesmerising about firelight and after a minute or two she wasn't really seeing it. She was seeing that fateful Friday evening, about a fortnight after his father's funeral, when Reid had come to visit her.

She'd noted his preoccupied air of sadness as soon as he'd arrived and she'd assumed that it was a natural expression of his grief, so she hadn't minded when he didn't pull her in close to kiss her as he usually did the moment he entered her house.

In the past their passions had run so high they'd often rushed straight to her bedroom. Later they would join the locals at the pub for a counter tea, or they'd prepare dinner together, sharing stories about their week, sharing laughter and kisses as they peeled and chopped vegetables, happy in the knowledge that a long night of loving stretched ahead.

On this particular Friday night she had tried to jolly Reid out of his bleak mood by reciting all the amusing anecdotes and gossip she could think of while she bustled about preparing dinner. But he had sat on a stool in her kitchen, gazing through the window, hardly showing any reaction—even when she had told him about Suzy Meyers bringing her grandmother's false teeth to school for show and tell—and how Johnny Johnson had stolen them at lunch time and tried to use them to eat his lunch.

Finally, when their dinner was in the oven, she had crossed the kitchen and slipped her arms around Reid and kissed him lightly on the mouth. For the first time ever, he hadn't returned her kiss.

Puzzled and more than a little scared, she had drawn back so that she could look into his eyes. And what she had seen had truly frightened her. The loving warmth had gone. It was as if the Reid she knew had been replaced by an alien.

'Reid, what's happened? There's something terribly wrong, isn't there? What is it?'

Dragging in a deep, tortured breath, he closed his eyes as if he couldn't bear to look at her. 'Everything.'

'Everything?' Truly frightened now, she plagued him with questions. 'What do you mean? Are you sick? In trouble? I know you're grieving—'

Lurching to his feet, he strode away from her. On the far side of the room he turned, and with his hands at his hips and his jaw squared, he watched her through cruelly narrowed eyes. 'Sarah, this is tough, but I'm going to have to ask you to back off. I need space.'

She almost collapsed beneath the shock. Reid wasn't making any kind of sense. How could a man who had always been so considerate and thoughtful suddenly behave in such an uncaring manner? How could everything have gone so terribly wrong? Surely she deserved some kind of explanation?

But it hadn't come, not then or in the years since. Reid had walked away that night without staying for dinner and he'd completely disappeared from her life for a month or two. And then, ever so gradually, he'd reinvented himself as her friend, a big brother—a boy next door type. And, fool that she was, she'd accepted these small crumbs.

She'd hung on because by then her love for him was so deep-seated and enduring that she had little choice but to go on loving him—from a distance.

'A penny for your thoughts.'

His voice startled her, pulling her back from the past to the fire, to the dark bush and the wind rustling through the treetops. He sat half in shadow, half in ruddy fire-light, but she could see that he was watching her carefully.

'I was thinking about you, Reid.'

His response was a scowl as he stretched out a leather boot and kicked a smouldering log back into the heart of the fire.

'I was thinking of all the questions I should have demanded answers to years ago.'

Even in the half-light she could see his sudden tension. He stood quickly and walked to the ute, returning with their pack-ets of sandwiches. 'Time to eat,' he said.

This was how it would always be. More evasions.

She refused to take the packet he held out to her. 'I'm not hungry.'

'You'll need strength to continue the search on foot in the morning.'

The masculine logic of his words and his complete inability to sense what was upsetting her broke the limits of her patience. 'I need strength to put up with your company for a whole night,' she snapped. 'But food won't help. It would make me sick.'

To her dismay Reid didn't protest. He nodded slowly. 'I can't blame you,' he said as he placed the packet of sandwiches on her swag. Then he straightened. 'I'll take a look around the area and leave you in peace for a while.'

Turning abruptly, he walked quickly away from her into the black night.

Aghast, Sarah jumped to her feet, but already he'd disappeared.

CHAPTER SEVEN

REID plunged into the night.

He thrashed his way through the under-growth, gripped by a sense of wild desperation. What a fool he'd been to try to kid himself that he and Sarah could spend a night alone—especially out here where the stars, the silent darkness and the campfire's glow seduced them with teasing memories of their passionate past.

His mind was tormented by self-recrimination as he marched in wide circles, keeping a discreet distance from her without losing sight of her fire.

Hadn't he put her through enough pain? He should have talked her into staying back at the homestead tonight—in Heath Drayton's tender care. He should have moved heaven and earth to facilitate her separation from his own bad company.

And now he'd made things worse by storming off when Sarah was trying to get an honest answer from him. What a bastard!

The knowledge that he'd hurt her too many times stabbed him like a knife thrust. He'd been a fool to think that his suffering in noble silence had spared Sarah pain. In reality his silence had caused her endless anguish.

He had to put an end to it. He had to tell Sarah the truth about his father tonight. In fact he would do it now, this very moment, before he came up with another crazy reason to back down.

I'm not worthy of you. I'm the son of a rapist. This is why you have to turn your back on me and leave the valley.

His insides churned as he swung to the left to cut straight back to their campfire. But in the same instant something in his peripheral vision caught his attention. Had he imagined it, or was there another faint light glowing in the opposite direction?

Standing very still, he studied the dark bush and picked up the glimmer of a fire about half a kilometre away. Could it be the boy?

Cupping his hands to his mouth, he shouted, 'Danny? Is that you?'

The night was very still and as he listened carefully he fancied he heard a faint reply. Excited now, he took a quick check on the position of the other fire before hurrying back to Sarah.

She was standing with her back to the fire, waiting for him. 'I heard you call. Have you seen Danny?'

'I'm not sure, but there's another fire further over. It could be other searchers, but there's a chance it's him.'

'It's got to be him. I couldn't bear it if it's not.' In the fire's light he could see the tension in her eyes.

'Sarah, there's something I need to tell you.'

'About Danny?'

'No…about…the past.'

'Oh.' Her eyes widened further, showing a mixture of fear and curiosity, but then she sighed and gave an impatient shake of her head. 'Not now, Reid. We've got to find Danny. Let's get going.'

He winced at the bad timing. 'Are you sure you wouldn't prefer to stay here while I go?'

'No way. I'm coming with you.'

She'd already collected a torch from the ute and as they plunged back into the dark bush she switched it on.

'It might be easier to pick up the glow of the other fire without that,' he told her.

'But I've been staring into the fire and I can't see a darn thing out here.' Just the same, she flicked the torch off again.

'Here—take hold of my hand.'

He expected a snapping retort but he offered her his hand anyhow.

In the stillness of the night her silence seemed to deafen him. And then, 'Okay, just till I get my night vision.'

She slipped her hand inside his and a jolt of heat scorched through him, stealing his breath. It had been so damn long since he'd held hands with this woman; he wanted to keep her hand linked with his for ever. Her hands were slim and finely boned, soft and feminine. So many times they had driven him wild.

Stop it, man. Don't let your mind go there.

'Should we call Danny again?' she asked.

'Good idea.'

Together they yelled Danny's name several times, then paused to listen. This time there was a faint but definite response.

Sarah clasped Reid's hand tightly. 'Did you hear that? I hope it's him. It's got to be him.'

'You can see the other fire directly ahead.'

By now her eyes were adjusting to the darkness and she let go of his hand and began to jog. He ran beside her, ducking beneath undergrowth and weaving between trees.

'Danny!' she called. 'Danny, are you there?'

As they neared the fire they saw a small huddled shape silhouetted against the flickering red backdrop.

'Danny?' Sarah called, rushing forward. 'It's me. Miss Rossiter.'

The shape rose. Reid saw thin arms and legs and then a small frightened face before the boy was enveloped in Sarah's arms.

She hugged him tight. 'Oh, Danny, I'm so glad we found you. Everyone's been so worried.'

The boy clung to her, but there were no tears. 'I was trying to find you,' he said in a rather matter-of-fact little voice.

'Find me? Why would you look for me out here?'

'I was walking into Mirrabrook.'

'Heavens, Danny. You couldn't possibly walk all that way. It's too far.'

With his cheek pressed into her shoulder, he said, 'They said you're going away.'

'I'm not going anywhere just yet,' Sarah reassured him. 'And I'm here now, so you must stop worrying.' She hugged him again. 'Wow, look at the beautiful fire you've made.'

'I brought matches and water and a pocket knife just like you told us to.'

'I'm proud of you, Danny.'

Reid's throat constricted as he watched the two of them—the slim, dark-haired woman with the small boy. He was mesmerised by the sight of her soft white hand lovingly stroking Danny's hair. This was how she would be with her own children. She would be the perfect mother of a cute little boy or girl—that he could never father.

Oh, hell. How on earth could he tell Sarah the truth? If ever there was a woman who deserved to be a mother, Sarah did, but she was so compassionate that she would be prepared to give up that right. She would offer to marry him in spite of his dark inheritance. But how could he do that to her? Instead of setting her free, the truth would bind her to him.

How could he think, even for a moment, that he should burden her with his terrible secret? He had to step right back from this beautiful young woman's life.

Oh, God. For a harrowing instant he doubted his ability to carry on in a world without Sarah. He'd been shouldering an unbearable burden on his own for too, too long. But he had to. He had to go on alone. It was the only fair thing to do.

Suppressing a groan, he turned away from them and switched on the radio so he could relay their good news to Heath Drayton.

They drove to Orion. Danny rode huddled beside Sarah and for most of the journey she remained silent. Before long, the boy fell asleep with his head on Sarah's lap, but the adults didn't talk. They were almost at the homestead when she turned to him.

'You said you had something you needed to tell me.'

'I did?'

'When you came back to tell me about Danny's fire.'

He shook his head. 'I've forgotten now.'

With a huff of irritation she closed her eyes and bit her lip. Then he heard her sigh. 'Are you sure, Reid? It seemed important at the time.'

He pretended to give the matter some thought and then shrugged. 'No, sorry, whatever it was, it's gone.'

She released a longer sigh which managed to convey the message that she didn't believe him, but Danny stirred in her arms so she didn't pursue the matter.

And as soon as Reid had delivered them both at the homestead he left Sarah to sleep at Orion while he pushed on, driving through the night, back to Southern Cross, where he could avoid further contact with her.

A week later Jessie McKinnon came home to Southern Cross and, to Reid's utter dismay, she brought her sister Flora with her.

'Why didn't you tell me Flora was coming?' he hissed at Annie when the two women had gone to their room to freshen up after their long journey.

'I thought you knew,' she snapped back.

'You never mentioned it, Annie. I had no idea.'

'So what? Why make a big deal of it? Flora's family. She's our aunt. I'm really thrilled that she's come all this way for my wedding.'

'But it would have—would have been *helpful* to know these things.'

Annie let out an irritated huff. 'Give me a break, Reid. You'd soon tell me to get lost if I tried to share every tiny detail about this wedding with you. I've had so much to think about—hiring the marquee, the caterers, the musicians and the photographer—finding accommodation for all our guests and getting everything ready for the ones who'll be staying here.'

Reid nodded and let out a weary sigh. 'I know I'm not pulling my weight.'

'That's not what I meant,' protested Annie. 'You've got a cattle station to run. Besides, you've always shouldered the responsibility here, ever since Dad died. You have plenty on your plate.' Cocking her head to one side, Annie eyed him shrewdly. 'But there's something the matter, isn't there? For the past week or so you've been edgier than a razor blade.'

He avoided her gaze, not prepared to answer that question.

'Well... I guess I'm getting edgy too,' Annie said. A wan smile flickered at the corners of her mouth. 'I seem to be missing Theo more than I thought I would.'

Her face softened when she said Theo's name and Reid marvelled at the miracle that love had worked on his tearaway tomboy kid sister. 'It won't be long now,' he said gently. 'And then Theo will be yours for a lifetime.'

'Yes.' Looking down at her engagement ring, she gave it a little twist so that the diamonds flashed and her smile grew warm and wistful. Reid thought she'd never looked prettier. But when she looked up at him again her eyes grew momentarily thoughtful and then unmistakably sad. 'Reid, I wish you could be as happy as I am. Kane has Charity and I have Theo and you deserve to be just as happy.'

To his horror he felt as if he might cry. 'I'm perfectly happy.'

'I wish I could believe you.'

'For God's sake, Annie, you're looking at the world through rose-coloured glasses. Believe me, not everyone needs to be married to be happy. I certainly don't. I'm not marriage material.'

'What makes you say that?'

The sound of footsteps in the hallway saved him. Jessie and Flora came into the room.

'Now we've shaken off the dust and we're ready for action,' Jessie said, smiling.

'I'll go and see if afternoon tea is ready,' Annie told them. 'Reid has found an absolutely fantastic cook, so I'm totally spoiled these days. Wait till you taste Rob's tea cake.' As she hurried off in the direction of the kitchen she called over her shoulder, 'Reid will look after you.'

Reid took a deep breath as he faced his two mothers; the one who'd adopted him and was so dear to him and the stranger who'd given birth to him.

The sisters were very alike, both attractive, with hair that had once been blonde but had turned to silver, and with light blue eyes like Annie's. Flora was taller and slimmer than Jessie and, because she'd only spent a short time in Australia, her face had fewer lines.

No doubt she had been very attractive when she was young, but Reid couldn't allow himself to think about that. He'd steeled his mind to block thoughts of what had happened to her all those years ago when she was young and pretty.

'Please, make yourselves comfortable.' With a dignified sweep of his arm he indicated the deeply upholstered armchairs and thought how strange it felt to treat Jessie McKinnon like a guest when she'd been mistress of this household for over a quarter of a century.

But it was even more unnerving to have Flora sitting here in the Southern Cross lounge room, her hands twisting nervously in her lap as she smiled just a little too brightly, while she expressed unnecessarily lavish admiration for the antique furniture, the landscape painting on the wall and the cut glass bowl of home grown roses that Vic the gardener had picked that morning.

Her Scottish accent seemed to accentuate her difference and her eyes darted about the room, apparently delighted by everything she saw. Everything except Reid. Whenever she looked at him her eyes took on a kind of troubled wariness, as if she needed to study him but was afraid of him.

And Reid, who had always prided himself on his ability to put people at their ease, found it a struggle to discuss even the most banal topics like the weather. He was relieved when Annie and Melissa came into the room carrying trays. At the same moment the telephone rang.

'Can you get that, Reid?' Annie asked.

'Sure.' There was a phone on a small side table and he crossed the room and picked up the receiver. 'Southern Cross. Reid speaking.'

His greeting was met by silence and then, 'Oh.'

'Hello.' He said it again, more loudly, 'Hello?'

'Reid.'

'Is that Sarah?' The unexpected sound of her voice sent a spike of electricity streaking through him. He hadn't seen her or spoken to her since he'd returned from Orion a week ago, but there'd hardly been a moment when he hadn't thought of her.

'I—I was hoping to speak to Annie,' Sarah said.

'No problem. Annie's right here. I'll get her for you.'

'But I may as well tell you,' she said quickly.

'Okay.' He struggled to keep his voice casual. 'What's the message?'

'My transfer's come through.'

Her news shouldn't have surprised him, but he felt suddenly winded, as if a fist had thumped him in his solar plexus. 'I—I see. That—that's good news. Where are they sending you?'

'To Alexandra Headlands on the Sunshine Coast.'

'Well, that's great news, isn't it? You'll be near your parents.' Sarah's parents had sold their property and retired to the coast three years ago.

'Yes. Mum's thrilled. I'll—I'll be leaving Mirrabrook at the end of term.'

He swallowed. 'When—when does the term end?'

'A week after Annie's wedding.'

So...in just two short weeks she would be gone.

'So, you're—ah—going to live at the beach?' Reid drew a quick breath. 'That's great. It'll make a nice change. You'll have a ton of fun there.'

'Yep.'

'I'll pass on the good news to Annie.'

'What good news?' asked Annie in the middle of pouring tea.

Reid looked back over his shoulder to find every woman in the room—his sister, Melissa, Jessie and Flora—watching him. Still clutching the receiver, he willed his facial muscles to dredge up a smile. 'Sarah's transfer has come through.'

'Oh, Reid,' Annie said softly.

Hell, the last thing he wanted was his little sister's sympathy. Especially not now in front of Jessie and Flora. He hoped they couldn't see the fine tremor in his hand as he held out the receiver to Annie. 'Here, you come and talk to her.'

To his relief, she handed a cup of tea to Flora and came to the phone.

'Here's Annie,' he told Sarah. Then he turned to the other women. 'Please excuse me.'

Melissa, having taken over Annie's role as hostess, smiled at him. 'Wouldn't you like some tea?'

'No, thank you.' Reid cleared his throat. 'I have to go and check the levels in some of the water troughs.' He hurried out of the room as if the hounds of hell were at his heels.

Sarah, on the other end of the phone line, felt ill. The simple act of telling Reid that she was definitely leaving had been so much worse than she'd expected. Her nerves were as tormented as the phone cord she was twisting between anxious fingers.

'Hi, Sarah,' came Annie's voice and it was good to hear her friend's warm cheeriness. 'Can you hang on a tick? I'm going to take this call from the study.'

'Sure.'

Twenty seconds later she heard Annie's voice again. 'Here I am. This is better. We can talk properly now.'

'I was just ringing to pass on the news that I've been transferred to the Sunshine Coast.'

'Lucky you. It's a gorgeous part of the world. All those beaches and cute surfing guys.'

'I know. It's really beautiful there.'

There was silence on the other end of the line and Sarah's nerves tightened a notch. Raking her free hand through her long hair, she sifted the silky strands anxiously. In her experience there was never so much as a moment's silence during a conversation with Annie McKinnon. What was her friend thinking?

'Are you absolutely sure that this is the right thing?' Annie asked at last.

Sarah drew a deep breath. 'Annie, I'm certain I have to do this.'

'I suppose you must be convinced, or you wouldn't have written the letter *and* that answer to your own agony aunt letter.'

Sarah couldn't hold back her gasp of surprise. 'Did you know I wrote the answer?'

'I didn't know it at the time, but I worked it out. Ned Dyson told me he was hunting for someone new to answer the letters, and I realised that both you and Ask Auntie were leaving town at the same time, so, knowing how clever you are, it wasn't hard to put two and two together.'

'Oh, crumbs. I wonder who else Ned's spoken to. Was he hoping you'd take over from me?'

'Heavens, no. But Sarah, couldn't you keep writing the column? Ned could email the letters to you.'

'No, I'm bowing out of that job.'

'But you've been so good at it. I even wrote to you once for advice, you know.'

Sarah smiled. 'I know.'

'Really? You guessed it was me?'

'You asked for advice about an Internet date.'

There was a stunned silence and then Annie said, 'That just goes to show how wise you are, Sarah. I wouldn't have met Theo if you hadn't encouraged me to go to Brisbane.'

'I'm glad it worked out well for you, Annie. But I've had enough of that job. How can I go on pretending to be wise when I've made such a hash of my own life?'

'But is running away the answer?'

Sarah flinched. It wasn't the answer she wanted, but what choice did she have? Deep down she longed for advice from someone else, someone wise, someone who could look at her problem from a fresh perspective. She'd shouldered her lonely heartache for so long now that she couldn't see the wood for the trees.

'I don't know, Annie,' she admitted. 'I suppose running away is a bit of a gamble, but then life's one big gamble, isn't it?'

CHAPTER EIGHT

WORD of Sarah's transfer spread quickly. The Mirrabrook School Parents' Committee decided to host a big farewell function for her, but there was also a flood of invitations to dinner in the homes of families throughout the district.

In the schoolroom she spent a lot of time talking up the new teacher, urging her little brood to look on the change-over as an important learning experience, a part of growing up. It must have worked because over the next week even Danny Tait became less agitated.

At home she kept herself busy, either packing six years of her life into boxes or fielding questions from her mother when she telephoned.

'I'm so excited,' her mother kept saying. 'It'll be lovely to have you living nearby.'

This was an improvement on her earlier calls. Until a few days ago Judith Rossiter had been trying to persuade Sarah to move back into their apartment. But Sarah had been independent for too long. Her parents had been in their forties when she was born and, although her arrival had apparently been a delightful surprise, they'd never quite adjusted their thinking to understand the younger generation.

'I've never understood why you wanted to bury yourself away in Mirrabrook for so long,' Judith said now.

'For the same reason you lived on Wirralong for thirty years.'

'But I was married, dear.'

Strained silence followed, and then her mother asked, 'What about Reid? How does he feel about your transfer?'

'I don't know. I haven't really discussed it with him.'

There was a dramatic sigh on the other end of the line. 'So you've wrecked your chances with that lovely man?'

'Mmm.'

'Young people these days have such a throw-away attitude to relationships.'

Now it was Sarah's turn to sigh. 'I guess we do, Mum.'

Right up till the day of Annie's wedding Sarah made sure she kept super-busy. She didn't want to let her mind become idle even for a moment. She'd done all the thinking she could bear and now it was a matter of getting on with the next chapter in her life.

On the morning of the wedding she woke early and continued packing crates with textbooks and knick-knacks until it was time to have a bath and to shampoo her hair.

Lunch was a hurried sandwich while she packed an overnight bag with make-up and the brand new lacy pink underwear she'd bought to wear with her bridesmaid's dress, along with pyjamas and a change of clothes.

It was an hour's drive from Mirrabrook to Southern Cross and, like many of the guests, she would be spending the night at the homestead after the reception. There would be a dozen or more fold-out stretchers set up on the verandas to cope with the overflow.

It was a beautiful day, perfect for a wedding, with cool and crisp air and high, clear, cloudless, cerulean skies. As Sarah drove she tried to focus on Annie's happiness and not on the fact that soon she would be back in close, torturous contact with Reid. Just thinking about how handsome he would look in his dark groomsman's suit brought her out in a cold sweat.

If her mind dwelt for even a second on a picture of the two of them walking arm in arm, sitting at the head table together or dancing, she felt a surge of sheer panic.

But, heaven help her, underlying the terror was the magnetic pull of helpless attraction, the insatiable hunger for Reid that had never faded. By the end of Annie's wedding she would be a mess of shredded nerves.

When she arrived at Southern Cross the paddock set aside as a car park was already cluttered with vehicles and the gardens were a hive of activity. A huge white marquee had been set up on the front lawn and hired waiters were setting the tables with starched white tablecloths, rose-pink serviettes and shining silver, china and glassware.

Down the centres of the tables fragrant deep pink frangipani flowers and tealight candles floated in shallow glass bowls of water. Vic, the Southern Cross gardener, was busy draping trails of white bougainvillea, pretty as bridal veils, around the marquee's support columns. By dusk the setting would be as enchanting as a fairy tale.

Sarah climbed the steps of the homestead's front veranda and was greeted by Annie's flushed and excited mother.

'We've banished the men in the wedding party to one end of the house,' Jessie told her. 'Annie and the bridesmaids are at the other end.'

She quickly hustled Sarah to Annie's crowded bedroom where she was immediately caught up in the high-octane excitement.

The blissful bride and Melissa were having their hair styled by Victoria, another bridesmaid, one of Annie's city girlfriends, who'd come armed with the very latest fashion tips from Brisbane.

Victoria took one look at Sarah and decided that her long dark hair must be fashioned into an elegant twist, with deep pink ribbons and white orchids positioned just so. And, when she'd finished, Sarah had to admit she was very impressed. Victoria had created a sophisticated hairstyle that managed to look careless and glamorous at once—and surprisingly feminine and sexy.

So of course she immediately wondered what Reid would think of it. *Idiot.*

The afternoon continued in a happy blur as the girls painted their nails with matching polish, applied make-up more carefully than they ever had before and then slipped into their beautiful dresses in varying shades of pink, while Jessie and Flora fussed over Annie.

Sarah gasped when she saw her friend in her dreamy sheer veil and her exquisite bridal gown of white Italian lace. 'Oh, Annie, what a truly gorgeous dress. You look absolutely radiant—the perfect bride. Poor Theo's heart will burst with pride when he sees you.'

'I'm the one who's bursting,' bubbled Annie. 'I think I might die if I have to wait another minute to see Theo.'

But Annie didn't have to wait because her brother Kane appeared at her bedroom doorway to announce that it was time. Time for Annie to link her arm through his and to

process with her bridesmaids along the veranda to the side garden where a string quar-
tet was playing and the wedding guests were
seated and ready. Sarah's heart began a
quickstep.

*Concentrate on Annie and Theo. This is
their day. Forget about you know who.*

But the lecture she gave herself was of
little use. Her bouquet of pink stargazer lil-
ies began to tremble as soon as she saw the
three men standing in line with Theo. Her
hapless eyes flew straight to Reid and a
river of sweet longing flooded through her.

He looked breathtaking. So tall and
darkly handsome. His broad shoulders and
tapered waist showed his beautifully cut suit
to perfection and she was awash with emotion as she walked behind Melissa to the
floral arbour that Vic had spent months preparing for Annie's special day.

She tried not to look Reid's way again,
but with the helpless compulsion of a sun-
flower following the sun her eyes kept seek-

ing him out. She was an instrument tuned perfectly to his pitch. And then their gazes met...

Oh, heavens. From beneath spiky black lashes his silvery-grey eyes shimmered and for a harrowing moment Sarah thought she saw the flash of tears. She felt a jolt in her chest as if her heart had fallen from a high place and smashed on to the ground like fragile glass.

How would she ever get through this? At the best of times weddings brought tears to women's eyes. Everything conspired to touch the emotions—the heavenly music, the beautiful flowers and romantic gowns, the blinding love shining from the bride and groom.

Concentrate on Annie and Theo. Pray for their happiness. This is their day. Fill your heart with love and good wishes for them.

To her relief, she found that when the ceremony began Annie's radiant joy and Theo's unmistakable devotion eclipsed her own silly fears. She was able to focus completely on their moving declarations of love and their exchange of vows and, to her everlasting relief, she didn't cry. If she'd started she mightn't have been able to stop.

But afterwards, when she had to link her arm through Reid's and walk back with him through the rows of seated guests, her discomposure returned with a vengeance.

She'd expected that he would break the tension by greeting her with a humorous comment or a joke as he took her arm. At the very least, she'd thought he might smile. But he said nothing and when he looked at her she was startled by the banked desire in his eyes.

A new wave of longing swept through her and quickly she dropped her gaze. In a week she would be gone from the valley, and her feelings for Reid, keenly sharpened by the poignancy of the occasion, were more foolish than ever.

It helped that the wedding reception was a very informal, relaxed, country-style affair. The musicians switched to playing popular tunes and the guests mingled, happily chatting, while photographs of the bridal party were taken in the garden and on the front steps.

Luckily Sarah didn't have to spend the whole time with Reid. Lots of people wanted to talk with her, to wish her well for her move to the coast, and she welcomed their distraction.

Dusk approached, accompanied by a background chorus of birdcalls as corellas and parrots winged their way homewards across the reddening sky. Down by the creek crickets cheeped. And under the floodlit marquee the floating tealight candles flickered romantically. The sweet scent of frangipani and the tinkling laughter of happy guests floated on the evening air as a delicious meal was served with a minimum of fuss.

Sarah, who was seated beside Reid for the supper, tried to tell herself that this evening was no different from the countless social occasions she'd attended as his partner. Except...

Except that this was the last time. And this time she was acutely aware of Reid's tension. He was as tightly wound as the coiled springs inside a clock and his talent for putting other people at ease seemed to have vanished completely.

They were fortunate that Victoria was sitting on the other side of him; she was talkative enough to keep everyone at their end of the table entertained. But, too soon, the dinner and the speeches were over and the dancing began.

Fine tremors vibrated all over Sarah as she stood beside Reid within the semicircle of guests and watched a beaming Annie and her gorgeous Theo perform the bridal waltz on the timber floor laid down at one end of the marquee.

'My little sister looks very happy, doesn't she?'

She turned towards Reid and almost sobbed when she saw the dark emotion storming his face.

'I've never seen a happier bride,' she said, her voice choking with suppressed tears.

As the best man and chief bridesmaid joined Annie and Theo, Reid tapped Sarah gently on the shoulder. 'You will dance with me, won't you?'

She gulped and nodded. It would be sweet torture but how could she refuse with so many people looking on? And how could she refuse when, despite the dangers, it was what she wanted to do more than anything else in the world?

She glanced at the smiling guests and saw Reid's mother watching them.

'Let's go,' she murmured and she hooked her little finger with his and together they walked on to the dance floor.

Her heart began to pound wildly and her body thrummed as she turned to face him. His eyes smouldered with sexy heat and she wondered, God help her, if she would ever find a way to stop loving him. His touch scorched her as they took up a dancing position with one of his hands at her waist and the other enfolding her fingers as if they were fragile treasure.

A corner of his mouth quirked into the faintest glimmer of a smile, but it flickered then vanished like a small candle flame extinguished by a gust of wind.

This should have been easy. They had danced together many times in the past and they were used to each other's rhythms and foibles, but this evening they were both stiff and awkward as they tried to move to the music.

Other guests were joining the dancers now, so they were no longer quite so obviously in the spotlight, but none of Sarah's tension eased. Instead, a thousand sweet memories and a dreadful, agonised longing assailed her.

Here she was in Reid McKinnon's arms for the last time, breathing the familiar scent of his skin and his aftershave. All her life she would never forget that special woodsy smell. She was breathless inches from his broad chest, his lean hips, his powerful loins.

She could remember in vivid detail every muscular inch of his long, hard body and she was forced to close her eyes as hot tears stung the backs of her eyelids.

As they continued to dance she felt his hand beneath her chin, and her eyes flashed open as he tipped her face so that he could look into her eyes. For five long heart-stopping seconds they gazed at each other—and Sarah felt a chill from head to toe. She knew she was looking straight into Reid's heart, stripped of the protective shield he'd worn for too long.

She could see his love for her and his gut-wrenching despair and—oh, help—his silver glittering tears. Oh, God, she couldn't bear it. Deep in her heart she'd always known that Reid loved her, but here was the evidence in his eyes.

She'd hung around all these years because of this. She knew that despite Reid's withdrawal from her they shared powerful emotions, a deep-seated, enduring love.

No matter how hard they'd tried to label their feelings as respect and friendship, they still took great joy from setting eyes on each other, from talking to each other and from just being in each other's company. No matter how often they'd pretended to deny it, the passionate hunger still burned.

But now it was all going to end.

Helpless tears slipped down her cheeks and when Reid saw them he emitted a strangled groan before gathering her close against his pounding chest. And Sarah clung to him, weeping silently, letting her broken heart have its way, while happy wedding guests waltzed around them.

'Who's that young woman dancing with Reid?' Flora asked as she and Jessie sat in a corner of the marquee enjoying coffee and wedding cake as they watched the dancers.

Jessie eyed her sister thoughtfully. She and Flora had always found it difficult to talk about Reid. Since they'd arrived at Southern Cross she'd wondered when Flora would finally pluck up the courage to raise the subject of her son. Instead it had been Annie who'd wanted to discuss him.

Despite being caught up with wedding plans, Annie had plied her mother with questions. To Jessie's dismay, Annie had confided that she thought Reid had been covering up a deep unhappiness ever since Cob's death.

It was disturbing to realise that she'd been guilty of negligence towards the dear boy. She'd blithely assumed that she could return to Scotland confident that he'd adjusted to the news of his adoption. But now she feared she'd been hiding her head in the sand by staying away for so long.

'That's Sarah Rossiter,' she told her sister now. 'She's the local schoolteacher.'

Flora nodded. 'She seems very nice.' After a bit, she added wistfully, 'Reid's a fine young man, isn't he?'

'He's the best there is, Flora.'

'He and Sarah seem very close.'

'Yes,' Jessie agreed as she watched the young couple dancing very slowly. Indeed, Reid and Sarah seemed lost in a world of their own, dancing with their eyes closed while Sarah's head nestled against Reid's shoulder and his cheek pressed against her hair.

She let out a deep sigh. 'Those two have been very good friends for years, but nothing's ever come of it and now Sarah's applied for a transfer and she's moving away, so I suppose whatever they've had is over.'

'You wouldn't think so to look at them now.'

'No,' Jessie agreed solemnly.

'Do you know why Sarah's leaving?'

'I can guess.'

Flora looked puzzled. 'Can you tell me? Have they had an argument? Is there a problem?'

Jessie frowned at her sister. 'I suspect Reid is resisting marriage. I think he'll always remain a bachelor, don't you?'

'Why should he? He seems perfectly wonderful marriage material to me.'

'But Flora, surely you can understand his dilemma?' When her sister continued to look puzzled Jessie's patience snapped. 'Wouldn't you agree he must be worried about passing on his father's bad genes?'

Flora gasped and her face turned chalk-white.

Jessie leaned close, speaking softly, urgently, so as not to be overheard by people sitting nearby. 'Are you all right? You look terrible.'

'Oh, dear,' whispered Flora and her eyes stared blankly in a kind of dazed horror. 'What have I done?'

'What do you mean?' Jessie struggled to fight off a mounting irritation with her sister. 'You haven't done anything. What happened to you wasn't your fault. You were a helpless victim.'

'But if Reid thinks—'

Flora covered her face with shaking hands and Jessie sat very still, watching her with bewildered concern. After a minute or two the other woman seemed to recover a little and she picked up her coffee cup and took a deep sip.

'I don't want to spoil this lovely evening,' she said. 'But I need to speak to Reid some time soon.'

'I'm very pleased to hear that,' said Jessie quietly. 'You and Reid haven't even acknowledged your relationship, let alone come to terms with it. While you're here, you need to make your peace.'

'Yes,' Flora said, but then she looked frightened again and her coffee cup rattled against its saucer.

Jessie tried to reassure her. 'Don't worry, Flora. Reid knows the worst about his father, and he's handled it in his own way.'

Her sister's mouth trembled. 'But he doesn't know the truth, Jessie.'

'What on earth do you mean?'

'He doesn't know what really happened.' Flora looked ill. She dropped her gaze to her lap where her hands were twisting in anxious knots. 'And, Jessie, I'm afraid you don't know the real story either.'

CHAPTER NINE

SARAH'S tears had made a damp patch on the front of Reid's shirt and she was sure her eye make-up had smudged. How embarrassing. Any minute now the music would stop, the dancing would finish and everyone would see her face.

'Do you have a handkerchief?' she asked Reid as they continued dancing close.

'Yes.' He patted his trouser pocket. 'Flora brought tartan-trimmed handkerchiefs from Scotland for all the men in the wedding party.'

'Bless Aunt Flora. I think I'm going to need to borrow yours.'

Tipping his head to an angle that allowed him to see her face, he smiled gently. 'Perhaps we'd better go outside.'

'Good idea.'

191

They left the marquee with her head resting against Reid's chest and his arm around her so that his bulky shoulder shielded her from curious eyes. When they reached the shadowy garden he turned her towards him and tilted her face so he could see it in the moonlight.

'How am I doing?' she asked in a voice that was deep and husky with emotion.

His mouth twisted into a rueful smile as he tried to dab at the skin around her eyes with his handkerchief. 'I'm afraid you're a bit of a mess.'

She bit her lip. 'Sorry.'

'Don't apologise, Sarah.' His voice sounded choked and shaking and suddenly he was pulling her close again, wrapping his arms around her as if he feared she might disappear into the night. 'You have no reason to apologise.'

Oh, God, his whole body was shaking. Crushed against him, Sarah could feel violent tremors shuddering through him, as if a dam was bursting, releasing all the emotions he'd held back for too long.

A shiver that had nothing to do with the night air feathered her skin and she reached trembling fingers to touch his cheek. 'Reid,' she whispered. 'You know I still love you.'

A terrible groaning sob broke from him. 'Oh, Sarah, what am I going to do?'

Dear God. Surely his heart-rending plea confirmed her fears; whatever had come between them was beyond his control. But it didn't matter. Nothing could matter now, not if they both acknowledged their feelings.

'Kiss me,' she murmured and she pressed her lips to the underside of his jaw. 'Kiss me, Reid. Kiss me.' She trailed frantic little kisses over his chin, all the way to his mouth.

But, to her dismay, there was a sudden burst of noise beside them and a loud party of laughing guests streamed out of the marquee and into the garden.

'Hey, Sarah. Annie and Theo are about to leave.'

A desperate low curse broke from Reid and Sarah was so awash with emotion she feared her legs might collapse beneath her.

From the home paddock came the chugging sound of a helicopter landing to whisk Annie and Theo away on their honeymoon. Reid released a shaky sigh as he took Sarah's hand. 'We'd better say goodbye to the happy couple.'

'Of course.'

More guests were spilling out of the marquee now and Reid kept holding Sarah's hand as they joined the crowd of well-wishers gathering around the newlyweds.

'Do you know where Theo's taking Annie for their honeymoon?' she asked him.

'I believe this chopper's taking them straight to an island resort on the Great Barrier Reef.'

'Lucky things.'

'Yeah.' He glanced her way and through the dark his eyes flashed silver heat.

Another shiver shimmied over Sarah's skin—a shiver triggered by thoughts of honeymoons—and the electric current arcing between herself and Reid. Minutes earlier, he'd been a heartbeat from kissing her.

Or had he? Perhaps she was getting carried away? No doubt her imagination had been overexcited by the romance of Annie's wedding.

Steadied by these thoughts, she hurried forward to kiss Annie and Theo goodbye and she made a big show of joining in a rousing cheer when Melissa caught Annie's bouquet. And she cheered as loudly as anyone else when they waved the happy couple on their way.

But, as the chopper lifted off, she turned to find Reid standing close behind her and she was certain he'd been watching her the whole time. Her chest tightened, squeezing the breath from her lungs.

'Okay, let's party on!' shouted one of the groomsmen.

Happy voices filled the night as the other guests drifted back to the brightly lit marquee.

Melissa, who was arm in arm with the policeman Heath Drayton, called, 'Are you coming, Sarah?'

Sarah looked back to where Reid was standing in the black shadows cast by a row of casuarinas. She fancied he shook his head at her, but perhaps that had been a trick of her imagination.

'I should go back,' she said to him, but her voice was low and shaky.

'Stay.'

The command was so abrupt it should have been insulting but, given her helpless obsession with him, she had little choice but to obey. A quick glance at the marquee showed her that Victoria and Melissa and their escorts had already disappeared. No one seemed at all bothered that she and Reid had remained behind.

He reached for her hand and his thumb rode over the backs of her fingers. 'Before we were interrupted, we were having a very important conversation.'

Sarah's face flamed.

'You were making a rather important request,' he said.

She'd been begging him to kiss her. 'Reid, don't make fun of me.'

'Why would I make fun of you?' He sounded so shocked her heart jumped and, before she could respond, he hauled her close. 'God, Sarah, you have no idea.' His hands framed her face. 'I can't resist you any longer,' he groaned into her mouth.

She wanted to tell him that he mustn't try to resist, but her answer was cut off as his lips sealed over hers—and at last, at long last—his mouth claimed her.

There was nothing gentle about his kiss. Nothing. This was unleashed desire at its hottest and fiercest. Reid took her as if he was staking a possession too long denied and Sarah was powerless beneath his assault. But she surrendered gladly, welcoming the bruising pressure of his lips and the urgency of his tongue.

She understood his need; she shared it. Her body burned with wanting him. As the black night enshrouded them she returned his kisses with equal hunger. They devoured each other.

Never had she experienced a passion like this. No words were needed. Their kiss communicated a message as old as time and, with a heady, thrilling rush of insight, Sarah suddenly knew that tonight there would be no stopping them. There would be no holding back.

This night would be theirs, stolen back from the dark fate that had kept them apart. They would pay no heed to whether this loving was right or wrong, prudent or sensible. They'd been practising restraint for too long and now this deep, elemental need had to prevail.

When kisses were no longer enough they turned and ran, holding hands as they rushed across the unlit lawn to the house.

Sarah's heart beat wildly as she slipped off her high heels and carried them so that her footsteps were soundless as she hurried with Reid to his bedroom at the far end of the long central passage.

Once inside, he shoved the door shut and her shoes tumbled to the floor as he hauled her to him, taking her mouth in another deep and greedy kiss.

Winding her arms around his neck, she pressed her breasts against him, anxious for the seduction of his teasing hands. Her hips rocked against his and she pushed into his arousal in an act of blatant provocation. She might have been shocked by her wantonness if she wasn't so aflame, so compelled by a wild, obsessive longing.

There were no whispered endearments, no tender avowals of love. Perhaps it was fear that kept them quiet, as if spoken words might break the powerful spell that held them in its thrall.

All Sarah heard was Reid's ragged breathing and the hushed swish of expensive suiting as he removed his coat and tie. With quiet efficiency, she took off her bridesmaid's gown and turned to him, dressed only in her new lacy pink bra and panties. And her heart almost leapt out of her chest when Reid sank to his knees in front of her.

Shirtless, he knelt at her feet and his silver eyes blazed through the moon-washed darkness as he touched her bare skin, tracing the curves of her waist with reverent fingers.

Then he bowed his dark head and kissed her.

Oh...

His lips touched her skin in an intimate caress that sent exquisite shivers trembling through her. She felt such a welling of love for Reid that her eyes filled with fresh tears. His tongue touched her, tracing tender circles and she felt so overcome with emotion and longing she thought she might collapse.

A soft, whimpering sound broke from her as she threaded needy fingers through his hair.

An answering growl sounded low in Reid's throat and suddenly he was bearing her upwards and on to his bed.

Together they tumbled, and Sarah savoured at last the precious luxury of Reid's body pressing close in a joyous full-length embrace. Oh, the bliss of his weight upon her, the giddy exhilaration of his skin, naked against hers. How she'd missed him.

They'd been cruelly apart for too long and now they shared a kind of panicky desperation as they helped each other out of the rest of their clothes. No more barriers.

Now…they were home.

Now…their hands and lips could take breathless delight in a rapturous journey of rediscovery.

This was her man, just as she'd remembered him, and this was where she was meant to be—sharing silken touches with him, giving and receiving kisses, daring kisses that knew no boundaries—travelling with him to the very limits of passion, and wanting the pleasurable torment to last and last.

Until…just when she reached the point where her body cried out for release… Reid rolled away from her and began scrabbling about in a drawer in his bedside table.

'What are you doing?'

'We need to use protection.'

A dark look crossed his face, torment behind his eyes.

'Don't worry. It doesn't matter.'

'Of course it matters. I've got to protect you.'

No doubt it was an irrational thought, but tonight felt like a night for taking risks. At that moment Sarah felt so reckless she welcomed an unplanned pregnancy. If she could carry Reid's child she would be linked to the man she loved, body and soul, for ever.

But he found what he was looking for and when he returned to the bed she had no choice but to cling to him as he took her with sensuous, passionate ardour. Together they soared high till their climaxes claimed them, shocking them with their shattering force.

And then they fell back to earth. Together.

They lay in the darkness and her head rested on his chest as she snuggled against him.

'Are you sleepy?' Reid asked, watching the way her eyes drifted closed as he dropped warm kisses on to her cheek.

'Only a little.'

He saw her drowsy smile and felt happiness roll through him like a hot wave, enticing his mind to play with the crazy fantasy that they were the bride and groom who'd been married today. This was their wedding night and now a long and happy future awaited them.

I love you, Sarah.

If only he could tell her. The thought burned in him. He'd loved her for so, so long.

This woman was so much a part of his soul he felt as if he'd loved her all his life— since a time long before they met.

Now...after tonight, he couldn't let her go without explaining that.

Without explaining everything...

'Sarah, we need to talk.'

Her eyes blinked open and she rolled a little away from him, as if she were trying to read his expression in the darkness. 'Will talking spoil what's just happened?'

Yes.

Heaven help him. That single syllable felt like a knife thrust twisting deep into his guts.

Yes... Telling Sarah the truth about his past, about his father, would spoil this beautiful night. After just a few words she would realise that this passion they'd shared could never be more than a parting gift.

How could he tell her that now, while she lay trusting and hopeful in his arms? Especially when, rising on to one elbow, she leaned towards him and kissed him gently on the mouth.

'I guess you're right,' she said. 'We should talk.' But she spoke with her mouth against his, and her lips wandered over his face in a soft invitation, mesmerising in its slowness. 'But maybe we should talk later,' she whispered.

'I don't know—'

'Let me make your mind up for you.' Her voice subsided to a low, seductive rumble as she moved over him and her silky soft curves made his blood pound as they brushed against his bare skin. 'Reid, I'm quite sure we should definitely leave the talking till later.'

He hadn't the heart or the will to argue with her… But then, later…after they made love again… Sarah fell swiftly and soundly asleep.

She woke at sunrise to find that Reid had left the bed and was standing at the window. His back was to her and he was holding the curtain aside as he stared at something in the distance.

She allowed herself a few moments just to lie there, admiring the godlike proportions of his powerful body, honed to taut strength by hard physical work. Her eyes lingered over the massive breadth of his shoulders, the smooth, sleek line of his back, the sexy curve of his buttocks and the muscular vigour of his long legs.

Oh, man. Last night this splendid creature had lavished her with his tender love and his magnificent passion. The way Reid made love to her had been physical and emotional evidence that her instincts had been right all along. He still loved her.

A ripple of happy warmth spooled through her and she felt quietly confident that at last, from this morning on, they would work things out. Surely last night was perfect proof that they were meant for each other. Everything between them was going to be okay.

She smiled possessively. 'Morning, gorgeous.'

He turned and his eyes gleamed when he saw her. He returned her smile slowly. 'Morning.' Crossing the room, he sat on the edge of the bed and reached for her hand. 'Did you sleep well?'

'Amazingly well. How about you?'

He shrugged and smiled again, but this time she thought she saw a shadow of sadness darken his eyes, like a cloud drifting over the moon. And, in a surprisingly modest gesture, he looped a corner of the sheet around his hips.

An unnerving shiver crept down her spine as she remembered that he'd wanted to talk to her last night.

'I fell asleep before we could have that talk,' she said and she propped up the pillows and patted the empty space in the bed beside her. 'Do you want to talk now?'

He remained on the edge of the bed, sitting some distance away from her, and his chest rose and fell as he sighed deeply. 'I don't really know where to start.'

She told herself that she mustn't panic.

Drawing on the courage she'd gained from the beautiful night they'd shared, she offered him a brave smile. 'You could start by admitting that you love me.'

'Sarah, I'm not sure it's wise to talk about love.'

'It's not wise to be honest? I think it's very important.'

'Wait till you hear what I have to tell you.'

'Okay.' She drew a quick breath, reminding herself again that it was vital to stay calm. If Reid sensed her fear he might retreat into silence again. 'I'm waiting.'

She tried to send him an encouraging smile, but he looked away and muscles worked in his throat as he swallowed.

'Perhaps you should have written a letter to the agony aunt,' she prompted gently.

'Yeah, perhaps I should have.'

'What would you have told her?'

Again he swallowed and, without looking at her, he said, 'That I have a terrible secret that will prevent me from ever marrying the woman I love.'

Her hand flew to cover her mouth, but it was too late to stop the horrified gasp that broke from her. Thank heavens Reid wasn't looking her way. She must have turned as pale as these bed sheets.

Taking another deeper breath she tried to stop her mind from racing ahead to imagine some terrible disease he might have contracted, or a secret wife and child hidden away.

'Reid,' she said, forcing her voice to stay calm. 'No secret could be that terrible.'

He turned to face her and his eyes were hard glittering stones. 'What if I were to tell you that I'm not Cob McKinnon's son?'

Her jaw dropped. Whatever she'd expected, she could never have predicted this. Reid was such an essential pillar in the McKinnon family; it was impossible to think of him as anyone but Cob's son. 'I'm—I'm not sure I understand.'

'It's true, Sarah. Cob was never my father.'

At first she couldn't respond. All she could do was sit there, mutely shaking her head. 'When did you find this out?'

'Just after he died.' His face contorted with pain.

'It must have been a terrible shock.'

'Don't worry, it gets worse.'

He jumped from the bed, crossed the room and jerked a wardrobe door open. Finding jeans, he dragged them on, and Sarah's heart sank. By getting dressed he was signalling the end of their intimacy; he was deliberately distancing himself from her.

With his hands on his hips, he stood scowling in the middle of the room. 'I shouldn't bear the McKinnon name,' he said through gritted teeth. 'Jessie isn't my mother, Annie's not my sister and Kane's not my brother.' His face twisted into a terrible parody of a smile. 'I don't belong here.'

'Are you telling me you're adopted?'

'Yes.'

She frowned. The news that Reid was adopted was a shock, but surely this wasn't his terrible secret? Lots of people were adopted. Something like that couldn't have been what had kept them apart all these years. It didn't make sense. She wanted to leap out of bed and throw her arms around him, but in the face of his renewed tension her nakedness felt wrong.

Tugging at the top sheet, she wrapped it around her, toga-style, and crawled on her knees to the edge of the bed. 'So what if you're adopted? You still belong here on Southern Cross. And—and we belong together.'

He shook his head. 'I'm afraid I haven't told you the worst of it.'

She couldn't bear to see his distress. Her heart trembled as she clutched the sheet over her breasts and waited for him to continue.

'I carry bad blood, Sarah.'

She kept her voice completely calm. 'What does that mean? Whose bad blood?'

'My father's,' he said without looking at her. 'My real father, that is. He—he—was a rapist.'

She knew Reid was waiting for her reaction but she remained absolutely still and quiet, and eventually he continued.

'My father raped my mother and then she gave me away because she couldn't stand the sight of me.'

Oh, God. Sarah's heart broke for him. This was the news that had hurt him so terribly. If only she could ease his pain.

She wanted to clasp him to her, to hold him with the gentleness of a mother. She yearned to comfort him as if he were a little boy, to rock him and soothe him until he lost the appalling cold hardness that filled him now.

Still gripping the sheet in place, she wriggled off the bed, but Reid jerked as if she'd already touched him and he whirled away from her.

'I can imagine how hurt you must feel,' she said to his back. 'Reid, I don't know much about the background of rapists, but I'm sure the cause isn't genetic. There must have been factors in this man's environment...'

He didn't seem to hear her. 'Can you imagine what it's like to know that every time my mother sees me she's reminded of the horror of my conception?'

It was too much. Launching across the room, she threw her arms around him. 'My poor darling. What an unbearable burden for you.'

To her dismay he rejected her efforts to hug him. He held himself stiffly in her embrace and eventually she had little choice but to release him.

'I'm sorry.' He spoke gruffly, punctuating his words with a shrug.

'It's okay,' she said. 'You have every right to feel angry.'

His jaw clenched as he bit off an irritated grunt. They stood in silence as long seconds ticked by.

'Reid, I can understand why you're so upset, but this doesn't have to be such a terrible problem. If it's any help, none of this makes any difference to how I feel about you.'

His eyes widened as he stared at her.

'I love you,' she reminded him gently.

He shook his head. 'You mustn't.'

A shaft of panic speared her. 'Reid, you're nothing like that man.'

'How can you be so sure? Last night I dragged you away from Annie's wedding. I lost my mind.'

'No more than I lost mine.' She tried to force a playful laugh. 'We were both a little wild.'

When he didn't answer she stepped in front of him again, waiting for him to make eye contact. At last he looked directly at her, his face almost devoid of expression, like the grey stone visage of a statue.

'Anyway, last night wasn't the only time you've made love to me, Reid. Think about all the other times.'

He closed his eyes quickly, but not before she saw the flash of anguish. She prayed for the wisdom to find a way to force him to face reality—not the crazy fiction his mind had invented. 'You've always been a considerate man, Reid. Passionate, yes, but never violent.'

He didn't respond but she knew he was listening. 'Last night I wanted everything you had to give me. I even wanted your baby.'

'No!' He lurched away from her to the window, and when he spun back to face her his face was dark with pain. 'Can't you see, Sarah? That's the problem. I can never give you a child. God knows how it might turn out.'

'There's every chance it would be the sweetest little baby ever born.'

'There's also a chance it might be a criminal.'

'I doubt that.' When he didn't reply, she asked, 'So you want to play it safe?'

His hands clenched into angry fists. 'Where you're concerned, yes. Always.'

'But Reid, life doesn't come with a safety net. Sometimes we've got to take risks.'

'I can't ask you to take this risk, Sarah. It's for the best that you're going away. Then you can forget about me.'

She stared at him in horror. 'You don't mean that.'

'Of course I do. You have to leave for the new school at the coast just the way you planned.'

'But last night—'

'Forget last night. It was a mistake. It should never have happened.' A muscle jerked in his cheek. 'I'm sorry. My behaviour was unforgivable. I've been weak and I've let you down, but you still have to go.'

'Reid, I love you.'

A raw, tortured look of pain racked his face and then he jerked his gaze sharply away and she knew he was fighting tears. God, so was she. Inside she was crying rivers. But she was too scared to allow herself the luxury of breaking down.

This was war and she had to win it.

'I can't marry you, Sarah.' His voice grated with a frightening edge of finality. 'I won't marry you. I won't burden you with my genes.'

'You're so wrong, Reid. I love you,' she repeated.

There was no answer.

'Reid, we don't have to have children. We can have each other.'

'No!' He raked a hand through his hair and dragged it down over his agonised face. 'I knew you'd want to be noble about this. That's exactly why I've never told you before. You're the kind of woman who's made for motherhood.'

'Not if it means losing you.'

He glared at her. 'I'm never going to ask you to sacrifice your right to be a mother. Somewhere in the future there'll be lucky kids who'll have you as their mum. That's the way it's got to be.'

Her stomach lurched then dropped as if she'd stepped off the end of a gangplank. 'Can't you get it through your thick head that I want *you* more than your baby?'

For a brief astonished moment hope shone in his eyes and Sarah thought he was going to give in, but then he shook his head again. 'You can say that now, but in the future you will regret it.'

She felt faint. She was losing this battle. No matter what she said, Reid was determined to reject her.

Lifting her chin, she squared her shoulders. She had one last piece of ammunition.

'Are you still trying to pretend that you don't love me?'

He lifted his hands in a gesture of vexed helplessness. 'This isn't a time to be talking of love.'

'Really?' She was surprised by how cold and in control she sounded. Inside she was falling apart. 'I can't imagine a situation where love would be more relevant.'

But he could be just as cool and controlled. 'Sorry, Sarah, you'll just have to accept that the topic is closed.'

'Reid, this isn't an Oxford debate. Our lives are at stake. Our happiness.'

'My point exactly.' Crossing the room, he showed no emotion as he opened his wardrobe door again and selected a shirt, jerked it off its hanger and held it out to her. 'You look uncomfortable in that sheet. Put this on while I go and fetch your things.'

CHAPTER TEN

REID rode like a man possessed. It wasn't his habit to force a horse to the limits of its endurance, but despair pushed him towards that barrier.

Today, as he galloped away from the homestead and towards the distant hills, he was on a quest for speed and danger and pain. If it were feasible he would ride straight off the edge of the earth.

He longed for oblivion, but that wasn't possible. The least he could hope was that the pounding of his stallion's hooves on the hard earth would drown out the memory of Sarah's voice telling him she loved him.

If he was lucky the cloud of white dust stirring beneath him would clog his nose and mouth and block out the smell and the taste of her.

But there was little he could do about the pictures in his head. He'd spent years trying to erase images of Sarah naked and lovely and wanting him. But after last night they were scorched indelibly into his senses. They would always be with him, forever driving him beyond the edge of reason.

And he had been unreasonable with Jessie. She'd been shocked when he'd announced that he was heading off into the bush for a few days.

'But we have a house full of visitors,' she protested. 'Many of them are your friends. What will I tell them?'

'Make something up,' he growled. 'Tell them there are fences down. A bore's broken. Half the herd has escaped.'

'Reid, this is because of Sarah, isn't it?'

He refused to answer her, but he knew that the truth was obvious. This morning Sarah had left Southern Cross without speaking to anyone or waiting for breakfast. And, within half an hour of her leaving, he'd been filling a backpack with supplies and saddling a horse.

'I wish you wouldn't go,' Jessie implored him. 'Flora was hoping to have a word with you.'

'Flora?' It was difficult to keep the scorn from his voice.

'Yes. She has something she wants to tell you—to tell us both, actually. It's about your father.'

'No, thanks. That's an information overload I can do without.'

'You never know, Reid. It might be important.'

He actually laughed at her then. 'If Aunt Flora—'

'Your mother,' Jessie corrected gently.

'If she had important news, why would she wait for over thirty years to pass it on?'

That stumped poor Jessie. Her face crumpled and he felt like a prize heel.

'Look, I'm sorry,' he said, 'but I really have to get away for a day or two—maybe longer.'

'Until Sarah Rossiter's left Mirrabrook?'

He nodded. 'I have to keep my distance from her.'

'Unlike last night?'

Reid flinched.

'You didn't dance with anyone else,' Jessie said, as if she felt compelled to defend her observation.

He let out a long, tired sigh and looked away.

'I thought when I saw you dancing last night that you and Sarah might have sorted everything out.'

'Yeah, we did.'

'But poor Sarah has taken off and you're looking the worst I've ever seen you. Whatever you sorted out, it can't have been very satisfactory.'

'Life doesn't come with a satisfaction guarantee.' As he said this he recognised that he was putting his own twist on Sarah's words. *Life doesn't come with a safety net.*

Jessie placed a hand on his arm. Once, she would have hugged him, but these days she was more cautious. He couldn't blame her.

'Reid, I'm so worried about you. What's happened? What's gone wrong? You used to be such fun. Remember all the pranks you'd get up to with Kane? This house was always so full of fun and laughter. I can't bear to see you so unhappy.'

'Nothing's wrong.' He sighed. 'Nothing that can't be fixed by a few days in the bush. Please don't worry about me. I just need to get away.'

And he walked away from her then, marching off to the horse paddock without looking back.

There was a mountain of last minute paperwork for Sarah to sort through before she could leave. Semester reports still had to be written, and the next term's budget had to be prepared. She needed to leave background information on each pupil too for the new teacher, and there was a stack of departmental paperwork to file or to send away to Brisbane.

Luckily her employers recognised that as both principal and classroom teacher she would need relief and a supply teacher was sent to take over her class for two days while she closeted herself in her office.

Actually, the title of office was too grandiose a term for the tiny airless room at the back of the schoolhouse. It was so small that by four p.m. on Monday afternoon there was hardly a surface that hadn't disappeared under mountains of A4 paper or manila folders.

But Sarah was grateful for the tedium of paperwork. Sorting through administrative minutiae kept her mind busy. For long stretches of time she could blank out thoughts of Reid.

And she'd made good progress on the first day, but now that it was almost over she felt dead tired. Sleepless nights, busy days, stress, stress, stress. By the time she reached the coast she'd be a wreck.

If only she could crawl home, nuke a quick snack in the microwave and try for an early night, but this evening she had another farewell dinner—with Ned Dyson this time. It was a blessing not to have to cook, but these farewell dinners weren't easy. Ned and his wife had become like family to her and saying goodbye wouldn't be much fun at all.

As she filed yet another folder she heard footsteps approaching through the school-room and then a woman's voice.

'Oh, dear, I'm afraid we're disturbing you.'

Turning, she was shocked to see Jessie McKinnon and her sister peering around the doorway. Her silly heart clattered.

'H-hello,' she stammered, unable to cover her surprise. She struggled to smile. 'Excuse the mess. My—my office isn't always like this.'

From the doorway Jessie said, 'We knew you'd be busy, Sarah, so we waited until school was finished, but it looks as if you're still snowed under.'

Sarah was too flustered by their sudden appearance to answer with anything but the truth. 'Actually, all these files make me look much busier than I really am. I'm nearly done for the day.'

Clearly heartened by this, Jessie took a tentative step into the room. 'If you're not too busy then, would you mind if we had a word with you?'

Yes. Of course she minded. She needed to put as much distance between herself and the McKinnon family as she could. An unexpected visit from these women had to include news of Reid and she was quite sure she hadn't the strength to deal with it.

'No, of course I don't mind,' she said, and she cursed inwardly. Here she was, once again letting her weakness for Reid interfere with common sense.

Jumping to her feet, she made a sweeping gesture to indicate the mess and she forced a smile. 'There's no room in here. We'd better go through to the schoolroom.'

Nervous flutters danced in her stomach as she led the way. She wondered if she should have invited the women next door to her cottage, but her house was littered with storage boxes and she sensed that this wasn't exactly a social call. She hoped it would be over quickly.

They sat facing each other in a triangle of adult-sized chairs that loomed extra large in comparison with the low chairs and desks of her small pupils. Sarah wished she was still behind her own desk. At least then she would be able to wipe her nervous hands on her skirt. 'Now, how can I help you?'

She addressed her question to Jessie and, as she did so, she realised that neither of her visitors looked any calmer than she felt.

Jessie leaned forward, hands clasped tightly in her lap, and her face looked pale and strained, her eyes tired and underlined by shadows.

Flora looked on with anxious blue eyes that were a perfect match for her sister's.

'Sarah,' Jessie began, 'there's no point in beating about the bush. I'm afraid we have rather a demanding request. You see, Reid has ridden off into the back blocks. I think he's camping out in that cave in the hills.'

Sarah swallowed. 'The Cathedral Cave?'

'Yes, I'd say so. Our problem is that Flora and I have something extremely important to tell him, but we can't reach him.'

'What about Kane? Can't he fetch Reid for you?'

'No, he and Charity needed to go back to Lacey Downs straight after the wedding. And I'm afraid Vic's too old to drive all the way out to the cave and our new cook's not familiar with the territory.'

Sarah tried again to clear the lump in her throat. 'Reid won't be out there for long. He'll be back soon, won't he?'

'It might not be soon enough,' Jessie said with a surprisingly dramatic air.

Sarah frowned. 'Is this an emergency?'

'More or less.' Jessie bit her lip and her shoulders lifted in a self-conscious shrug. 'It's important that we speak to him before you leave.'

Sarah's heart gave an almighty thump and she felt her face flood with colour. What on earth did this mean?

'I know it's a lot to ask,' Jessie added hurriedly. 'But Flora and I were hoping that you could go out to the cave. You're such a good horsewoman and you know the way. You could reach Reid in a few hours.'

Oh, God. Sarah's stomach tightened so fast she thought she might be sick. What were these women up to? Surely they weren't trying to matchmake? 'I'm sorry, Jessie. I can't.'

'I know you're busy.'

'Yes, I'm very busy, but even if I wasn't I couldn't go out there. I don't want to see Reid and he wouldn't welcome me.' She blinked away the threat of tears. 'He and I have said our goodbyes.'

Heavens, this was too much. She'd had enough of being at this community's beck and call. She'd gone the extra yard for the McKinnon family. Couldn't people give her a break?

Reaching out, Jessie squeezed her hand. 'Sarah, my dear, Reid hasn't confided in me, so I can only guess why you and he are both so upset, but I believe Flora's news could set things right between the two of you.'

Flora's news? Sarah frowned. What on earth did Reid's aunt have to do with any of this? She shook her head. 'No, I'm sorry, it's not possible.'

'Sarah, I wouldn't be asking this of you if I didn't have your interests at heart. We'd both be so relieved and grateful if you'd try to reach Reid.'

'I *have* tried, Jessie. I've been trying to reach Reid for years. It's no good. I—I know when I'm beaten. I've had enough.'

She couldn't handle this. She'd been coping till now. Okay, maybe she wasn't eating or sleeping, but at least she'd managed to keep her tears at bay until after dark. But now she felt as if she might break down completely in front of Reid's mother and his aunt.

Jumping to her feet, she began to pace the floor, and she had to take several calming breaths before she could speak. 'Honestly, I don't think there's anything else I can do. Reid's told me about his—his *father.*'

She glanced back at the sisters and they were both frowning but she continued anyway. 'It doesn't matter how much I try to reassure him that I still love him, he won't listen. He's being incredibly stubborn. He's taken the high moral ground and he thinks he's doing me an enormous favour by turning me loose.'

Jessie sighed. 'He might change his tune if he knew the truth.'

The truth? Sarah's brow furrowed as she considered this. Knowing the rapist's identity wouldn't help Reid now. She doubted anything would reach him. He was too full of the hurt that was wreaking havoc inside him.

'He probably wouldn't listen to you. He's tearing himself apart emotionally, but I can't do anything. Every time I try to help he suffers more.' Sarah's mouth trembled. 'And I'm left devastated.'

Now Jessie was on her feet too. 'I'm sure Reid loves you, Sarah.'

Fighting tears, Sarah ploughed her hands through her hair. *Don't cry. Don't you dare cry.* 'That's the problem. I've clung for ages to the belief that Reid loved me—and he does.' With a brief despairing sigh she let her hands drop back to her sides. 'But at last I understand that love isn't enough.'

'Oh, no, my dear, you must be mistaken.'

Sarah shook her head. 'Love isn't everything. Romantics see love as a cure-all, but sometimes it takes more. It takes—oh, I don't know—a leap of faith.'

There was a loud gasp which seemed to come from Flora.

'I'm sorry, Jessie. I can't help you with this.'

Reid's mother stared at her for a long moment and then her shoulders slumped and her blue eyes took on an air of defeat.

It was almost dusk now and the dull light in the schoolroom seemed to magnify the bleakness of their conversation. The two women both looked so depressed, so bitterly disappointed, that Sarah felt a stab of alarm. Had she missed something here? When Jessie spoke about the truth, what exactly had she meant?

Could she be making a big mistake? Her mind whirled. Was the universe offering her one last chance?

'What on earth can I tell Reid that will change his mind now?' she asked suddenly. 'Can you give me one good reason why I should go to the cave?'

To her surprise it was Flora who responded.

Reid's aunt actually smiled, although it was a very wobbly smile and her eyes shone damply. 'I can do better than give you one good reason, Sarah. I have two.'

'Two?' she repeated in a shocked whisper.

Flora nodded and took a deep breath. 'You see, my first reason is that I'm Reid's mother.'

Sarah's jaw dropped. She couldn't have felt more shocked if Flora had announced she was an escapee from a faraway galaxy. She glanced at Jessie, who smiled awkwardly and gave a barely perceptible nod.

Flora continued. 'And the second thing is that I very much want him to know the truth about his father.'

'The man who—who raped you?'

Flora shook her head. 'I wasn't raped.'

Pow! Sarah felt as if she'd been slugged by an unexpected fist. Her head spun and she reached out to a nearby windowsill to steady herself. 'Reid believes you were—goodness, p-perhaps we'd better sit down again.'

'Thank you, dear. I'd like to explain.'

Sarah nodded. 'Yes, of course.' Her legs were like jelly as she crossed the room and turned on lights before they resumed their seats.

Flora, anxious now to tell her story, began without invitation. 'It's been very wrong of me to keep silent for so long,' she said in her softly lilting Scottish voice. 'I could offer excuses, but I won't take up your time with them. The truth is that Reid *is* Cob McKinnon's son.'

'Good heavens.' Sarah couldn't help glancing again at Jessie, who was sitting very stiffly, her face carefully masked by a gentle smile.

'You see,' continued Flora, 'I always loved Cob. For some time he courted me—before he met Jessie.' She and her sister exchanged a telling glance. 'I was very—very fond of him, but he chose Jessie. I'm not proud of what I did next, but I was so upset that a couple of weeks before their wedding I made sure that I had Cob for one final night—alone.'

Flora lowered her gaze and stared at the floor as she continued. 'Cob had too much to drink that night. It was his buck's party and I—we—I'm afraid we had a final—*fling* before—before I lost him for ever.' After a bit, she said, 'The—night—well it resulted in a pregnancy.'

'Reid,' Sarah said softly, and she sat very still as her mind absorbed the deeply emotional family secret that was unravelling before her.

'Yes.'

Sarah turned to Jessie, who smiled carefully. 'So why does Reid think his mother was raped?' she asked gently.

Jessie sighed. 'Actually, that was my fault. Flora wouldn't speak about the baby's father.'

And for very good reasons, thought Sarah.

'Poor Flora was on the verge of a nervous breakdown,' said Jessie. 'I knew there'd been a rapist in the district and I jumped to conclusions. The whole family did.'

It made sense. Thirty-odd years ago a pregnancy out of wedlock was considered shameful. Jessie would have been eager to defend her sister and happy to discover a simple explanation for her condition.

'I'm to blame for not having the courage to tell Jessie the truth,' admitted Flora. 'By being silent, I let her assume I was a rape victim. It was a way out—better than hurting my sister.'

'What about Cob? How did he handle all this?'

Flora chewed her lower lip and her eyes shimmered. 'Poor Cob—I felt so guilty. I begged him to swear he would never reveal the truth about my pregnancy. And you know a McKinnon—once he's given his word. It was a burden he carried for the rest of his life.'

Reaching into her pocket, she took out a handkerchief and wiped her eyes. 'I was sure I couldn't offer my son any kind of happiness,' she said sadly. 'So I asked Jessie if she would adopt him. We let everyone think he was Kane's twin brother.'

For a minute Flora looked as if she might break down and Sarah's heart went out to her, but then she gave a little shake and rallied.

'It seemed the best thing I could do for Cob and for my little boy,' she said. 'Reid could stay with his father to grow up in a loving family. I went back to Scotland and let everyone here get on with their lives.'

'How sad. You sacrificed your own happiness.'

Flora nodded. 'It was the hardest thing I've ever done, but it seemed the right thing to do at the time. Righting a wrong.' She looked up suddenly. Her eyes were dry now, but they were haunted by shadows.

Sarah sat very still, trying to get her head around this astonishing revelation. After a while she turned to Jessie. 'So you never knew?'

Jessie shook her head. 'I knew Cob wanted to tell Reid something important before he died. He was waiting for Reid to get back from a muster, but he—he ran out of time.' She smiled bravely. 'I must admit I'm grateful I never knew the truth until yesterday. I might have allowed it to wreck my marriage.'

But if only poor Reid had known...

As if reading Sarah's thoughts, Jessie said, 'Reid deserved to know long ago. I thought I did the right thing by telling him what I believed to be the truth about his mother, but I'm ever so sorry I told him about the rapist. But I thought it was the truth and he deserved to know.'

'Yes, indeed.' Sarah couldn't quite keep the bitterness from her voice.

'You can see why we wanted to contact Reid before you left town.' Leaning forward, Jessie's eyes implored Sarah. 'It's time he knew the truth. The real truth. You will go to him, Sarah, won't you?'

CHAPTER ELEVEN

REID woke, shaking with the vividness of his dream. Cob had been right beside him, looking tanned and healthy, streaked with sweat and dust, just as he always had when he came back from a hard day in the stock-yards.

In the dream he'd walked straight up to Reid and said, 'You're a damn fool, son.'

The vision had been so clear and the voice so real that Reid half-expected to find Cob standing beside him now, tall and strong as ever.

It took several moments before his eyes adjusted to the darkness and the reality that he was lying in his swag on the sandy floor of a cave in the side of a mountain. Alone.

He shivered and saw that his fire had almost gone out and as he stared into the faint glow of the few remaining coals his head wouldn't let go of his dream.

'I'm damn angry with you, son,' Cob had said. 'Twenty-nine years I put into bringing you up, but as far as you're concerned that counts for nothing.'

Reid frowned as he thought about that. What had the old man meant? Shaking his head, he reached for a stick to poke some life into the coals and he tried to forget the dream. Those words hadn't come from Cob. For Pete's sake, dreams came from your own subconscious. And they never made a lick of sense.

Sparks shot up as he stirred the coals. In a very short time the fire rekindled and he added more wood. Soon flames were leaping high, sending orange light dancing over the walls of the cave. He thought about boiling a billy for tea, but knew that if he wanted to get back to sleep he'd be better taking a slug or two of the rum he'd brought with him.

There was a small hip flask in his saddlebag and he found it and took a deep swig, noting with a kind of detached interest the way the fiery liquid spread down and through him. He drank some more, settled back on his swag and willed his mind to relax, to stop thinking.

But the words from the dream returned. *Twenty-nine years I put into bringing you up, but as far as you're concerned that counts for nothing.*

Releasing a deep sigh, he rolled on to his side and tried to forget the dream, but the thing was, dreaming about Cob had given him a brief respite from dreaming about Sarah.

Asleep or awake, he knew he would never be free of her, couldn't be free of the sight of her lovely face, or of her eyes and the agony that had filled them when he'd finally convinced her that there was no hope for them.

Those beautiful blue eyes kept haunting him, accusing him. And now Cob's voice accused him too. Hell. Why couldn't they leave him alone? Why should he still feel so damn guilty? He'd done the right thing by Sarah. He'd ensured that the sins of his father could not be passed on to another generation.

If only Cob… No! There was no point in thinking about *if only*. That led to madness.

Reid swore aloud and the rough oaths echoed back to him from the depths of the cave. Grimacing, he closed his eyes and saw Cob again. Had those twenty-nine years counted for nothing?

He sat bolt upright.

With the kind of clarity that came like a bolt from the blue, the words from the dream unravelled a knot in his thinking. *Hell! How had he missed it?*

Cob might not have been his biological father, but he'd overseen his upbringing.

That did count for something. It counted for a great deal.

Twenty-nine years I put into bringing you up...

As head of the McKinnon household Cob had gone to great lengths to make sure that Kane and Reid had grown into sons he could be proud of. He'd always figured in their lives as a large and powerful presence, someone the boys could count on—a strict but loving father, guiding by example.

Cob had moulded their characters, teaching them right from wrong. From him they'd learned loyalty, old-fashioned honour and self-respect. Cob had helped to mould his thoughts...his speech patterns. Reid had been told he even walked like Cob.

Reid shoved the swag aside and leapt to his feet. It was so obvious. He couldn't believe he'd been so blinded. He'd been fixated by the horror of having a rapist for a father and yet his childhood had been filled with happiness and stability. He'd been surrounded by positive images of manhood.

How could he have overlooked the powerful legacy of Cob McKinnon?

Rushing to the mouth of the cave, he stared out across the dark valley below and dragged in huge gulps of cool night air as he came to grips with this.

He'd thrown away his one chance at happiness with Sarah and he'd broken his darling girl's brave heart because he was horrified by the thought of his father.

But what if Sarah was right? What if environment counted for more than DNA?

No wonder she thought he was a coward. He'd rejected her offer to carry his child, to raise it and love it. And yet Jessie and Cob had knowingly taken on a potentially problem child, fathered by a criminal, and they had raised him with the same love they'd bestowed on their own children.

They'd taken the risk. For him.

Oh, God. Poor Sarah. She'd been willing to take a similar risk, but he'd been too afraid. He'd been such a fool. And now, through his own stupidity, he was losing her.

What the hell was he doing hiding out here? Moping?

Bloody hell! He had to find her.

Racing back into the cave, he bundled up his swag, quickly doused the fire with water and covered it with sand. Then he tore down the mountain to where his horse was tethered. With the last of the moonlight to guide him and with a sure-footed horse beneath him he could start now and reach Southern Cross soon after breakfast. Then he could grab a truck and be in Mirrabrook before Sarah had to begin teaching school.

When Sarah reached Southern Cross very early the next morning she didn't stop at the homestead; she went straight to the horse paddock to saddle up Jenny, her favourite mount.

She felt terrible. It was all very well for Jessie and Flora. They were certain that as soon as she reached the cave everything would be rosy. They expected that the minute she told Reid the good news that Cob was his father he would ask her to marry him and they would live happily ever after.

But Jessie and Flora didn't know how many times Reid had rejected her recently. She'd spent another sleepless night bombarded by doubts.

Now that she was actually on Southern Cross she tried to draw a little inner peace from the beautiful morning and the stillness of the bush. In the past the tranquillity of the outback had always worked its magic on her.

The Southern Cross saddling enclosure was built at the top of a rise and from there she could see a wreath of pretty white mist lingering in the little dip where the creek ran. Soon the mist would be chased away by the sun that was rising now like a dazzling globe in the east.

The lemon light of the sun slanted through the leaves of the big old gum tree, bathing the sheds and the yards with its warmth, and as Sarah adjusted the stirrups on Jenny a butcher bird called a sweet morning welcome from a branch above her.

She took a deep breath of clear morning air and willed herself to relax. Fat chance. She was terrified that telling Reid the truth about his father might not be enough. If, knowing that, he still wanted her to go away, her heart would shatter into a thousand pieces.

Once she had the saddle and bridle in place she stroked the mare's neck, hoping the action would soothe her own nerves as well as the horse. But Jenny was placid; there was no excuse to linger.

She flipped the reins over Jenny's head and was about to swing up into the saddle when she heard a new sound in the distance. The drumming of hooves.

All thoughts of staying calm vanished. Sarah abandoned Jenny and rushed to the fence. Leaning over the sliprail, she squinted against the sun.

At first the horse and rider coming out of the mist were no more than a black silhouette against the blaze of light, but as they came nearer she recognised Reid.

A force like lightning jolted through her.

Astride a black stallion, he came galloping up the grassy slope from the creek at a reckless pace and he looked so wild and wonderful that she wanted to weep.

Almost immediately her heart began to race as fast as his horse. She was suddenly terrified. Why had he come back? What if she made a mess of this meeting?

As he reached the yards Reid saw her. His horse came to a sudden standstill and he froze in the saddle, staring at her, and her heart seemed to jump and hang suspended in mid-air.

'Sarah.'

His eyes were shaded by his wide-brimmed hat, so she couldn't read his mood, but his mouth was unsmiling, almost grim. She tried to say good morning, but no sound came out. Oh, help. Her tension was unbearable.

'This is a surprise,' he said. 'Why have you saddled Jenny? What's going on?'

He seemed unhappy to see her. Her fists clenched as she steeled herself for the worst. 'Jessie needed me to ride out to the cave to find you.'

'Jessie?' His chest rose and fell as he digested this news, but there was no smile—nothing to give her hope. 'Why did she bother you?'

'Don't be angry with her, Reid. It's okay. I—I volunteered to find you for her.'

He shook his head. 'She shouldn't have interfered. I told her I'd be fine.'

'She—' Sarah gulped. 'She has some very important news. Actually, Flora has the news.'

He dismounted and looped the reins around a fence post, all the while watching her with a dark, unreadable expression.

His shirt was rumpled as if he'd slept in it. His jeans were old and threadbare, streaked with red dust and torn at the knees and his jaw was covered with two days' growth of black stubble. To Sarah he'd never looked more desirable.

But heavens, this was going to be even harder than she'd imagined. She'd pictured meeting Reid out at the cave—the two of them sitting beside a remote rock pool and surrounded by silent wilderness while she told him Flora's story. Now that he was home it would make more sense just to send him up to the homestead where Flora could tell him her news firsthand.

Perhaps she should just turn around and go back to town?

Reid walked towards her and his mouth twitched into the faintest suspicion of a smile. Taking off his Akubra hat, he set it on a fence post and with an unconscious sweep of his hand he ruffled his flattened hair.

'You've saved me a trip into town,' he said.

'Have I?'

He nodded slowly and for long seconds his eyes held hers. They stood either side of the post and rail fence, staring at each other. There was something different about him, something shimmering in the silvery depths of his eyes that she couldn't quite pinpoint. His gaze seemed to be drinking her in.

'Well,' she began and then she had to stop and run her tongue over her dry lips. 'You've saved me a long ride out to the cave.'

He nodded and the threat of a smile lingered in his eyes and about his mouth.

'Don't move,' he ordered suddenly, and with an agility that left her breathless he vaulted the fence to land neatly beside her. 'I can't believe you're still here,' he said, taking her hand in his. 'After all I've done to you, Sarah.'

His unexpected words and his gentle touch electrified her. 'I—I can't quite believe I'm here either. Call me stubborn.'

'Oh, Sarah.'

She looked into his eyes and saw an emotion so powerful it stole her breath.

'I'm the one who's been stubborn.' He reached for her other hand. 'I was coming to town to find you, to tell *you* something important.'

She gulped and felt so tense and scared and confused and in love she feared she might fall apart at any moment.

'Flora's message can wait,' he said.

'Are—are you sure? It's w-wonderful news about—'

'It can wait, Sarah. I need to tell you my news first.'

The authority in his voice silenced her. He clasped her hands and held them to his chest and she could feel his heart pounding as hard as her own.

'What did you want to tell me?'

'How much I love you.'

Oh, Reid.

She'd waited so long to hear those words and now all she could do was cling to him, bunching his shirt in her trembling hands, while her eyes and throat filled with tears.

'I love you, Sarah. I've been deeply in love with you for so long I can hardly remember a time when I didn't love you.'

She was so rocked by her rioting emotions she couldn't speak. She wanted to tell him how happy he'd made her, but all she could do was nod and smile at him as tears welled in her eyes and spilled on to her cheeks.

'Can you ever forgive me for being such a pigheaded fool, for denying my love?'

She nodded again.

'Can you understand how horrified I was that I would taint you?'

He looked so terribly upset she had to reassure him. 'Deep down I knew, Reid,' she whispered as her tears fell. 'That's why I hung around. All this time, I was sure you still wanted me.'

'I can't believe I've been such a stubborn fool. I've wasted so much of our lives.'

Weeping openly, she nodded again and pressed her lips together to hold back noisy sobs.

Reid gathered her close and kissed her wet cheeks. 'I'm so sorry, Sarah. We should have been together all these years, raising a family.'

A family? A little cry broke from her. Heavens, she had to get control. Taking a deep breath, she willed herself to calm down. She rubbed her damp face against his shirt and looked up at him with a teary smile. 'I can't believe I'm spoiling this lovely romantic moment by crying. I don't want to cry.'

His face was creased by a crooked grin. 'Believe me, sweetheart, having your lovely body shaking all over me is perfectly romantic. You can cry all over me any time you like.' He pulled her close again. 'Just so long as you're with me, Sarah. Hell, when I think of the needless pain I've caused you—how close I came to losing you—I want to cry too.'

He pulled back suddenly and his eyes looked worried. 'Do you have to leave? I know I've put you through so much misery I have no right to ask, but I don't think I could bear it if you went away. I don't think I can let you go, Sarah.'

She lifted her face to him and her mouth trembled as she smiled. How on earth did Reid think she could go now? Just the same, she couldn't resist a tiny tease. 'I'm not sure how the department will react if I tell them I've changed my mind because my boy-friend won't let me leave the district.'

'Perhaps you'd better tell them your husband won't let you out of his sight.'

'My husband?'

'You will marry me, won't you?'

'Is this really happening, Reid? I feel as if I have to pinch myself.'

His face broke into a beautiful grin. 'I promise you, it's for real, Sarah.'

'Could you just say it again, please, so I can be sure?'

'On my knees?'

'Oh, no. Heavens, no. Just tell me again about wanting to be married and having a family. Did I really hear that too? About babies?'

'Absolutely. I want hordes of our babies and there's nothing I want more in this world than to have you as their mother.' He kissed her tenderly. 'And as my wife.'

'I'd be honoured, Reid.'

'Oh, sweetheart.' Wrapping his arms more tightly around her, he hugged her in an iron grasp that thrilled her in its fierceness.

When he relaxed she looked up to see his rueful smile. 'It took a while to sink into my thick skull, but I know now that it doesn't matter that my father was violent, because our kids will have the sweetest, bravest, wisest mother in the world.'

His hands slid down her back. Fingers splayed, he coaxed her hips against him and his eyes burned with a smoky fire that melted her bones, and then his lips brushed hers in a gentle caress. 'And I'll be their dad and together we'll be the very best parents we can be.'

'Absolutely.'

'I love you so much, Sarah.' He scattered kisses over her face.

She remembered that she still hadn't told him her news. 'Reid, you don't have to worry about your father.'

'I'm not worrying about him. I only want to think about you.'

'Flora—'

Before she could tell him Flora's story, his mouth intercepted her. His lips sought hers and there was no way she would consider interrupting him. Happiness rained through her as he kissed her deeply, lovingly, binding her close again.

Savouring the powerful strength of his body, hard against hers, she remembered the day they'd stood in this very yard and she'd wanted him to do this, to haul her into his arms and to admit how he felt about her.

Now she submitted joyously, thrilled by the knowledge that at last Reid understood; their love was enough. He wanted to marry her, even though he still thought there were risks involved.

Just the same, when he'd finished kissing her thoroughly and when she'd taken her time to kiss him back just as thoroughly, she would take great pleasure in being at his side when he learned that Cob McKinnon, the father he'd loved, was indeed his own flesh and blood.

A month later the tiny wooden church in Mirrabrook was filled to overflowing.

Almost everyone in the community, whether they were invited guests or not, wanted to witness the wedding of Star Valley's beloved teacher to one of their most respected cattlemen. They all agreed there could never be a more fitting bride for Southern Cross.

People who couldn't find a seat in the church gathered on the footpath outside, or lined the streets to cheer Sarah as she arrived.

Wearing a dreamy fly-away veil and a simple fitted white silk gown and carrying a bouquet of exquisite white orchids, Sarah processed arm in arm with her father down the short stretch of the main street from her cottage to the church.

Annie, her matron of honour, walked on the other side of her, wearing a lovely gown in Sarah's favourite misty-blue.

No bridegroom was more keyed up than Reid as he waited at the front of the church and listened to the rousing cheers from the street. With him stood Kane, his best man, and the travelling bush padre, who'd made a special trip into Mirrabrook for this very important occasion.

Glancing behind him to the front pew, his eyes met Jessie's. He owed this woman so much. She'd mothered him with a generous and loving heart and, together with Cob, she'd made him the man he was today. She smiled at him now, but her mouth wobbled and he knew she was close to tears. Then he caught Flora's eye. Over the past few weeks he and Flora had begun the delicate process of getting to know each other as mother and son. He thought they'd done rather well.

To his surprise, she seemed very composed today. She smiled happily now and sent him a wink. He'd discovered that she was a woman of unexpected inner strength—like Sarah—and, sustained by that thought, he managed to smile as he returned her wink.

Through a side window he could see the churchyard and he thought of Cob lying out there. The news that he was Cob's son in every sense had brought him incredible joy and had taken an enormous weight from his shoulders, but there'd been bitterness too when he thought of the years of unnecessary heartbreak he'd suffered. However, with Sarah at his side, he was too happy to let anything cloud his joy for long.

Today, at Sarah's suggestion, they would leave her bridal bouquet on Cob's grave before they headed off to the Community Hall for their wedding breakfast.

A bell rang loudly. Danny Tait was in the front porch pulling the ropes to announce that Sarah had arrived. Kane placed a reassuring hand on his brother's shoulder. 'This is it,' he said. 'Turn around, mate. Here's your bride. She looks absolutely beautiful.'

Reid turned and a surge of emotion tightened his throat as he caught a glimpse of Sarah framed in the church's doorway. His vision misted. He couldn't help it. Here was Sarah. His life. His bride. Looking so lovely he couldn't breathe.

The congregation stood as the opening bars of the wedding march pealed from the wheezy old electric organ. Sarah had been talking to Annie, who was checking that the veil and gown were in order, but now she lifted her head, took her father's arm once more, and looked down the aisle clear to Reid.

Her blue eyes sparkled as she smiled. And his heart turned over.

He marvelled at how serene she was, and he remembered the first time he'd seen her, walking on to the school stage to make a speech. What a very special woman—this graceful, confident, darling girl walking to him now down the mercifully short aisle.

The picture of her blurred and he had to blink and take deep breaths.

Then at last Sarah was at his side. At last he could smell her perfume, hear the soft whispering rustle of her gown and see her face, looking lovelier than ever beneath the sheer veil.

'Hi there, handsome,' she whispered.

And finally Reid felt her touch as she slipped her arm through his.

'You look so beautiful,' he told her and he squeezed her hand as it rested against his coat sleeve.

They smiled into each other's eyes and Reid saw his deep love for this woman mirrored in her radiant smile—a beautiful, enduring love that had already been tested by time and trial and found to be lasting and true.

And his heart was filled with a sense of perfect happiness and promise as they turned to face the padre.

EPILOGUE

THE air rang with excited shrieks and peals of laughter as children played hide and seek in the dusky Southern Cross garden. On the veranda their parents sat in easy chairs, drinking sundowners and laughing, sharing jokes and generally catching up on all the news that was vitally important to no one but other family members.

Sarah looked around her and released a long, blissfully contented sigh. She'd never had brothers or sisters of her own and she especially cherished these times when the McKinnons got together.

None of them would have missed Reid's birthday. Kane and Charity and their three boys had driven over from Lacey Downs early this morning to help Reid and Sarah spruce up the homestead and garden so that

Southern Cross was looking its festive best for the big party planned for tomorrow.

Inside the house, the furniture and timber floors shone, the windows and mirrors sparkled and, thanks to the children's contribution, every doorknob was polished to a golden glow. Beyond the veranda, the newly trimmed lawns looked as green and smooth as city parkland.

Annie and Theo, who lived way to the south in Melbourne these days, had arrived late in the afternoon, absolutely glowing with pride and desperately keen to show off their brand new baby, their first-born.

'Trust you two to wait till most of the work is done,' Kane had joked as soon as everyone had duly admired sweet baby Thomas.

'Give me a break.' Annie wrinkled her nose at her brother, who still took every opportunity to tease her. 'Producing a Grainger son and heir is the hardest work I've ever done.'

'And that's coming from a woman who's just earned first class honours at university,' Charity reminded Kane.

Theo nodded vehemently. 'I was there in the delivery room and I'm in doubt about which was harder work.'

Annie cuddled her baby close and her face glowed. 'But Thomas was worth it, weren't you, little man?'

Now, as they sat on the veranda, Sarah smiled as she held her youngest nephew. She touched a fingertip to one of his tiny pink hands and watched it flutter like a flower in the wind. She feasted her eyes on his perfect little ears and the fuzz of his soft hair, and enjoyed the way he snuggled against her, so warm and soft and tiny.

Watching her, Charity smiled. 'Don't you feel clucky when you hold a dear little new-born babe?'

Sarah laughed and her eyes caught Reid's. This was something they'd been talking about recently and now he smiled and sent her a sly wink, stirring a happy coil of anticipation deep inside her.

'You might have a boy next time,' suggested Annie.

'If we have another baby, Reid will be hoping for another daughter,' Sarah told them. 'You're absolutely smitten with your girls, aren't you, Reid?'

At that moment there was a scream from the garden. Three-year-old Lucy's hiding place had been found and now she was fleeing across the lawn, squealing as she tried to escape her cousin Ben, Kane and Charity's youngest.

Reid grinned. 'I guess I must be smitten to contemplate another child after Lucy.'

Lucy, their younger daughter, had been a gorgeous but demanding handful from birth, and she'd developed a recent passion for baby animals that kept her parents shaking their heads. They'd found puppies in her bed, kittens dressed in dolls' clothes and chickens peeping from the pockets of her jeans. Heaven knew what would happen next time there were poddy calves that needed bottle-feeding.

Now, out on the lawn, cousin Ben was too fast for Lucy and, as he closed in on her, she squealed shrilly at the indignity of being caught.

'Time to restore the peace.' Reid jumped to his feet and loped down the steps.

'I think this is our cue to bring the children inside,' said Charity. 'Otherwise they'll be overexcited and won't be able to sleep tonight.'

'I'll bribe them in with hot chocolate and toasted sandwiches.' Sarah was already on her feet and handing Thomas back to Annie. 'We don't want them to be tired and cranky for the party tomorrow.'

The party was scheduled to begin late on Saturday afternoon and by four p.m. Southern Cross was ready and waiting.

All the vases in the house were filled with bright flowers from the garden—red and pink flowering ginger, purple bougainvillea, deep apricot frangipani and bright orange heliconias—a glorious riot of tropical colours.

French doors were opened wide to provide easy access for guests to wander between the lounge and dining rooms and on to the verandas, which had been made festive with bright streamers, balloons and strings of Chinese lanterns.

Extended tables were covered with pristine starched tablecloths and set at one end of the long lounge room to serve as a bar for the guests. In pride of place amidst the rows of polished champagne flutes and wineglasses stood a magnificent cutglass punchbowl that had been one of Jessie and Cob's wedding presents.

Now it was filled with rosy-gold punch and was being kept cold by a ring of ice set with pieces of pineapple, cherries and mint leaves.

In the kitchen Rob, the cook, was putting the finishing touches to the party fare.

And in her bedroom Sarah, having dressed her daughters in their new party frocks, was putting the finishing touches to her make-up. Nearby, in their *en suite* bathroom, Reid was standing shirtless before the mirror, shaving.

With a final flourish of her mascara brush, Sarah was satisfied and she walked through to the bathroom to check on Reid's progress.

Watching her reflection as she came into the room, his eyes took on an especially iridescent shimmer and he smiled at her. 'Wow, you look gorgeous.'

She was wearing an off-the-shoulder silk sheath in his favourite shade of blue—one that deepened the blue of her eyes—and she'd added glamorous dangling blue and silver earrings.

'You don't look so bad yourself, birthday boy, even though you're half covered with shaving soap.'

Standing behind him, she reached her arms around him and hugged his middle, which was as trim and taut as ever. In the mirror they shared a smile, a private, intimate smile, full of sexual promise. A ripple of joy bubbled through her as she thought about later tonight when they would be alone at last.

'You look so good I want to muss you up a little.' He looked down at her, still smiling. 'When are these guests due to arrive?'

'Any minute now.'

'Pity.'

Releasing him, she leaned back against the towel rail and watched as he finished shaving, wiped the last traces of soap from his face and slapped on aftershave. And as the familiar scent filled the small room, she remembered a time when she'd feared that the smell of this brand of aftershave would always bring terrible memories, reminding her of everything she'd lost.

Yet here she was, happier than she could have believed possible. She watched the play of his muscles as he reached for the shirt hanging on the door, and thought how amazing it was that her gorgeous husband loved her more with each year of their marriage.

After seven years of hard work running Southern Cross, after the ups and downs that had included the disappointment of a miscarriage followed by the joyous births of Jane and then Lucy, they shared a passion that always left her breathless.

Dressed now, Reid turned to her, drew her close and kissed her forehead. 'I don't dare kiss you anywhere else or I'll completely destroy your make-up.' He cupped her face and smiled into her eyes. 'I really do appreciate all the trouble you go to every year for my birthday.'

'It's fun. It never feels like trouble.'

Dropping a feather-light kiss on the tip of her nose, he said, 'I know why you do it.'

'I want your birthdays to be special.'

'Because I grew up never knowing the correct date I was born and having to share Kane's birthday?'

She nodded.

His gaze held hers. 'I love you, Sarah McKinnon. You're the finest woman I know.'

'The finest?'

'And the loveliest...*and* the sexiest.'

'That's better.' She kissed him lightly on the jaw. 'I love you, Reid.'

No longer caring about smudging lipstick, he lowered his lips to hers, and who knew what damage might have occurred if a sudden cry hadn't interrupted them.

'Mummy! Daddy! Come quickly!'

'That sounds like Jane.' Sarah sighed softly. 'I'd better go and see what's happened.'

'Daddy!' called their daughter again, sounding even more urgent. 'Hurry!'

This last cry was a quivering shriek that might have been excitement or terror.

They found Jane dancing a nervous jig in the middle of the lounge room, her eyes huge as she pointed with a shaking hand. 'Look.'

'Oh, no!' cried Sarah.

Reid let out a hoot of laughter.

Two black ducklings were swimming in the McKinnon family's heirloom bowl of fruit punch.

Sarah gave his arm a swift thump. 'Don't you dare laugh. The punch is ruined!'

'Oh, I don't know. Two little wild ducks cruising in a bowl of punch looks pretty artistic to me. We could start a new fashion.'

'Reid!' Sarah felt as if she wanted to strangle someone. 'This is Lucy's handiwork, isn't it?'

He was fighting an urge to smile. 'Probably.'

As they watched, one of the ducklings flipped its tail towards the ceiling and dived to the bottom of the bowl, while the other flapped its wings with excitement. Rosy-gold liquid splashed high and pieces of chopped fruit slopped over the edge of the bowl and soaked quickly into the starched white tablecloth.

'Now that's really artistic!' groaned Sarah. 'Look at the mess.'

'I only wanted to give the duckies a swim.'

At the sound of the small voice behind them, they whirled around to see Lucy marching into the room. Smudges of mud spoiled the front of her party dress and her sash had come undone and was trailing behind her.

'Oh, look at you!' cried Sarah. 'You've been very naughty.' She added this in her best ex-schoolteacher's voice.

'I'm sorry,' said Lucy, not sounding very repentant at all. She looked up at Reid and managed to squeeze one tear out of her big blue eyes.

'Where did you find these ducklings?' he asked her.

'In the dogs' water bowl.'

'That young Labrador pup must have brought them up from the creek.'

Sarah's hands lifted in a dramatic gesture of exasperation, but as she caught the merriment in Reid's eyes her sense of humour kicked in and she dropped them to cover her mouth as a chuckle threatened. 'Oh, dear, the poor things will be drunk if we don't get them out of there.'

'I'll take them through to the bathroom and wash them off with fresh water,' Reid volunteered.

Rolling back the sleeves of his white dinner shirt, he scooped up a duckling in each hand, extracting them swiftly and with a minimum of squeaks and splashing.

'You'd better come and help me, Lucy.'

Sarah watched him hurry away, with Lucy scampering to keep up with him, and she shook her head and sighed. Mad as she was about the mess, it was hard to stay angry. Lucy's naughtiness was never malicious and...well...she looked so much like Reid.

She lifted the punch bowl and, as she turned to carry it back to the kitchen, she heard a car door slamming outside.

Charity came into the room, looking lovely in a soft green trouser suit that matched her eyes. 'I think the first of your guests have arrived.' Her eyes widened as she took in the mess on the table and the bowl in Sarah's hands.

'Lucy's handiwork.' Sarah raised her eyebrows. 'Ducklings in the fruit punch. A new party trick.'

'Goodness.' After staring at it for several seconds, Charity grinned and shrugged. 'I can sympathise. Life's never dull when you're the mother of McKinnon kids, is it?'

Still smiling, she hurried to take the bowl from Sarah. 'I'll look after this. You've put in a huge effort for this party. I can have fresh punch made in a jiff. You go and greet your guests.'

'Bless you, Charity. You're a darling.'

'That's what I tell her every day,' said a masculine voice from the doorway. Kane entered the room and a quick smile flashed between him and his wife.

'You can make yourself useful, Kane,' Charity told him. 'Find a clean white sheet from the linen press.'

That settled, Sarah took a deep breath.

From the bathroom came a sharp quack and a delighted shriek from Lucy, followed by Reid's low voice, calm and stern, yet full of love. And from along the veranda rippled the bell-like tones of Annie's laughter as Jane gave her an excited report about the ducklings.

From the kitchen wafted the enticing aroma of bruschetta and tiny pizzas and, as she walked to the front door to greet her guests, she heard the clink of glassware as Kane and Charity went into damage control.

And Sarah knew that life was good. Her heart was light. The McKinnons were ready to party.

MILLS & BOON® PUBLISH EIGHT LARGE PRINT TITLES A MONTH. THESE ARE THE EIGHT TITLES FOR OCTOBER 2005

———— ❦ ————

MARRIED BY ARRANGEMENT
Lynne Graham

PREGNANCY OF REVENGE
Jacqueline Baird

IN THE MILLIONAIRE'S POSSESSION
Sara Craven

THE ONE-NIGHT WIFE
Sandra Marton

THE ITALIAN'S RIGHTFUL BRIDE
Lucy Gordon

HUSBAND BY REQUEST
Rebecca Winters

CONTRACT TO MARRY
Nicola Marsh

THE MIRRABROOK MARRIAGE
Barbara Hannay

MILLS & BOON®

Live the emotion

0905 Rom

MILLS & BOON® PUBLISH EIGHT LARGE PRINT TITLES A MONTH. THESE ARE THE EIGHT TITLES FOR NOVEMBER 2005

❦

BOUGHT: ONE BRIDE
Miranda Lee

HIS WEDDING RING OF REVENGE
Julia James

BLACKMAILED INTO MARRIAGE
Lucy Monroe

THE GREEK'S FORBIDDEN BRIDE
Cathy Williams

PREGNANT: FATHER NEEDED
Barbara McMahon

A NANNY FOR KEEPS
Liz Fielding

THE BRIDAL CHASE
Darcy Maguire

MARRIAGE LOST AND FOUND
Trish Wylie

MILLS & BOON®

Live the emotion

1005 Rom LP